NO LATHERING MATTER

A MAGICAL SOAPMAKER MYSTERY

S.E. BABIN

Copyright © 2021 by S.E. Babin

All rights reserved.

No part of this book may be reproduced in any form or by any electronic or mechanical means, including information storage and retrieval systems, without written permission from the author, except for the use of brief quotations in a book review.

Previously Published by Sweet Promise Press

KEEP IN TOUCH

If you'd like to keep up with new releases, please sign up for Sheryl's newsletter at sebabin.com. She only emails when she has a new release.

1

The sunset sent arching rays of orange light streaking across the darkening sky of Moonmist Springs. It was my favorite time of day - the time when people were busy cooking dinner or taking walks - or, in my case, pouring a difficult soap pattern. It was just me. No significant other or children running around. For the most part, it's a happy existence. Though it used to get pretty lonely.

Now I had a talking skeleton and a little mixed breed pup who only left my side for training. Sometimes I wished the dog could talk and the skeleton couldn't because Harry, the pile of bones watching me from the corner of my soap shed, talked all the time. There was rarely a moment when he wasn't chatting about something.

I guess if I was a skeleton and couldn't leave the house, I'd be chatty, too. Today he grumped about one of the customers I had. She was one of the more frustrating proprietors of my shop, The Suds Stop, though I never said so. As a small business, I needed all the customers I could get. Most of the time I did a brisk business. But even with money coming in, I still tread carefully when it came to potentially alienating anyone who came into my shop interested in my soap.

My soap was different from everyone else's. This wasn't an arrogant or over-reaching statement, though it may seem so. I was a witch who could infuse emotion into inanimate objects. So far I had no official name or title, no label magic users could put on me. I thought of myself as someone who could manipulate ambiance - the environment, animals, people, but I mostly chose to use my powers for good so I stuck to using it in my products and only for happy things.

The magic gifted to me made me uncomfortable at the best of times because it allowed me to feel everyone's emotions so strongly. If sadness came into the shop, I could tell. If someone was grieving, I knew it. If someone had just gotten a job promotion, I could feel it wafting off of them like a fine perfume.

I'd learned over the years to shield against a lot of it, but I chose not to shield completely. Being able to feel people's emotions made me quite the salesman, especially when I made products that could help them.

Anyhow, Harry, the animate skeleton I'd found when I'd been gifted this house in my mother's will, rambled on about Bree. His voice - crisp with a sharp British accent - droned on. "I can't believe she treated you so poorly. Really. I don't know why you put up with that kind of nonsense."

There was rarely a slight Harry didn't capitalize on. I couldn't see his emotions. He was a skeleton, after all, but his voice dripped scorn.

"She was having a bad day, Harry," I said, a slight touch of censure in my voice. "That's all. I didn't take it personally."

Harry scoffed. His bones clattered together in what I now thought of as his disgusted shudder. "It's always personal, Ivy. That woman hasn't had a good day since she moved to this town!" If he could have clucked his tongue, he would have.

I ducked my head to hide my smile at the visual. Harry was sensitive about his lack of organs and skin. I tried not to make it worse by teasing him. I slowly poured the chamomile soap colored black with activated charcoal into the creamy white of the main soap base. I was careful not to let it splash. The soap had barely traced so I could get all the beautiful swirls I was aiming for. I set the container down and picked up the bright yellow one, slowly pouring that one into the bowl, too.

"I choose to turn the other cheek," I told the skeleton as I worked. "I'm here to provide a service. She keeps coming in because she keeps having bad days." I shrugged. "So yes, she's a little mean to me, but she keeps buying my soaps." I looked up and smiled at him, finally at ease with his permanently grinning visage. "It's a win-win for me. It's the day she finally realizes she's the cause of her own misery that I may have to worry. Then we'll lose her business."

Harry eyed me, or at least I thought he did. It was hard to tell what he was looking at since he had no eyeballs. "Hmm," he said. "I suppose that's good logic."

I didn't hide my smile this time. I finished pouring the coppery brown soap and scraped the rest out with the flat edge of a spatula. I slid the wooden top on the mold and tapped it once for good luck. In 24 hours, I could unmold this batch and slice it open to see what it looked like on the inside.

It was one of my favorite soaps - infused with chamomile and lavender oils for peace and relaxation, but also made with activated charcoal for purifying the skin. I always tried to make sure my soaps did double duty. Emotions first, then skincare. Each had their own properties. Some were peaceful, some were uplifting, but all were wonderful for your skin. The way I made soap ended up both technical and magical. I made every single batch with proper amounts of lye, oils, butters, and other additives. The magic came from me. I infused every single step by focusing on what I wanted the current batch to have. For this one, I added the appropriate herbs and also infused it with thoughts of peace, calm, and relaxation. Anyone who bought these bars should feel the stress begin to lift away as soon as they used it.

"That smells wonderful," Harry remarked, his bones rattling as he found a more comfortable position. I still didn't get how he could smell things. He had no nose, after all. I shook my head just like I always did when he said something weird.

"I truly don't understand the magic animating you, Harry," I said with fond regard.

"I'm not sure the witch who made me did either," he mumbled.

Harry was prone to long periods of melancholy, though thankfully they only came every few months or so. I'd been here for a little less than a year and saw him twice spiral into depression. You've never seen anything like a depressed skeletal spirit. The last time it happened I threatened to roast his bones in the oven and use the marrow for my stew.

He looked scandalized at my descriptive torture methods. I was desperate for him to stop moaning about everything while I tried to work. It was effective, though. Harry, perhaps stunned by my willingness to go to the lengths I'd described, straightened up not too long after. It saved my sanity and several of my soaps. A rattling whiny skeleton wasn't so great for concentration when it came to trying to perfect a soap pour.

Harry came with the house and was so excited when I found him, he hadn't stopped talking since. I liked him, though. Despite his moodiness, I had to admire how quick and clever he was and had to give him credit for helping me to further hone my magic.

"Have you found anything else out about it?" I asked him quietly. The witch who made him was another sore subject with my in-house skeleton. He swore he couldn't remember much about her, but every once in a while, he'd make a comment to make me think maybe he'd known her quite well.

Ever since I'd known him, Harry had been trying to figure out the magic that animated him and how he could free himself from the confines of his skeleton. All I suspected was he was a spirit, though I didn't know what kind. He refused to tell me his age, but from some of his speech patterns, I estimated him to be at least 60-70 years old. He could be much older than that if he adapted how he spoke to modern times. But now that I was here and all moved in, he had free access to the internet and since we were living in Moonmist Springs, he could go outside and stargaze. Harry couldn't roam far from the property, though. We discovered this quite on accident when he was following me around outside as I foraged for wildflowers. Everything was fine one moment, but the next he'd stepped over some kind of invisible boundary and his bones collapsed in an enormous pile.

Talk about traumatic. I'd screamed bloody murder and tried fruitlessly to gather up his bones. I ended up skipping my gathering session, used the basket to transport him back home and laid him out on my soaping cabinet as I tried to figure out how to bring him back. I pored over all my spell books, called my sister in a panic, and when all that came to naught, I thought I might have to grieve for him.

I'd left Harry on the table and the next morning heard the familiar rattle of his bones as he stomped around the house. I'd never been more relieved to see a skeleton in my entire life. It was that moment I became a little more patient with his mood swings and a little more open to having an ... unconventional roommate.

Harry sighed. "No. Nothing. I thought it might be necromancy, but I struck out. I'm a spirit, not a body. He gestured to himself with a bony hand. "I mean, I have a body here, but I don't know if it's my own."

Considering he had *Property of Moonmist High School* emblazoned down one of his back ribs, I thought the odds of that were low. I'd never told him either. No one wanted to know they belonged to the science department for sophomore biology.

"Hmm," I said, noncommittal. I'd looked a few times for him as well, but I'd never found anything productive. Every lead I found died. We always came right back to where we began. At point zero with little information to go on other than Harry possibly being an animate spirit possessed of personality and intelligence.

I took a pile of dirty bowls, pitchers, and spatulas

over to the sink. Washing them now would be an exercise in futility because the soap hadn't fully formed so it would be like washing an oil slick. If I left the dishes for a couple of days, the soap mixture would harden making them a lot easier to clean.

"I'll see if Holly knows anything." I'd asked her before, but my sister made scatterbrained seem like a desirable trait. She was so above and beyond scatterbrained I thought it slightly a miracle she managed to dress in clean clothes every morning. In spite of it all, she was wonderful. Sweet, intelligent, imaginative, and she could bake the best bread I'd ever tasted in my life. Where I worked with emotions and ambiance, Ivy worked with the land. She had the greenest thumb I'd ever seen and she joked that the land in Moonmist could sense when she was fertile because flowers would sprout up around her feet if she happened to walk on it barefoot.

That one always made me wince, but she wasn't wrong. I'd seen it with my own eyes. She was like a little land nymph, flitting from one flower to another, keeping the land alive with her touch. I was a little jealous of her because I really had to work at it to keep my plants alive. When she came over, I didn't have to water anything for a week and I swore the air quality went up by at least twenty-five percent. Holly's fascination with Harry charmed the old skeleton and, if I didn't know any better, I'd think he had a crush on her.

Did spirits get crushes? Questions like that gave me a headache.

"Holly?" Harry said, his voice steady - too steady. He never missed an opportunity to chat about my sister.

"Mmm-hmm," I said, turning away so he wouldn't see my amusement. "She'll be over in just a few minutes." I stripped off my goggles, rubber apron, and gloves, and thoroughly washed my hands. I'd been making soap and body products for so long I had it almost down to a science now, but every so often I ended up with a mess. I'd gotten a lot more careful about keeping my gloves on through the entire process now, too. Once the oils and lye water mixed together, the soap making - or saponification - process started right away. It wasn't as dangerous as straight lye water, but if I got the mixture on my skin, it still stung.

"Oh," Harry said. He stood abruptly. "I'll be right back." He clomped out of the room, and I let the grin fully form on my face. Every time Holly came over, Harry got a little ... ridiculous. The last time she visited, he'd worn a necktie and suit jacket which made me laugh out loud. I still didn't know where he managed to rustle one of those up considering I had never had a man in my house.

The doorbell rang as soon as I finished putting away all of my oils. There was still more needing to be done, but it could wait until after I'd visited my sister.

As soon as I opened the door, I had to smile. Holly was small, dark-haired, and cute as a button. Her eyes were the color of quicksilver and her expressive face just made her that much prettier. Her features were fine, if not a bit sharp, but her kind eyes and ready smile dulled the edges of her narrow face and put her into more classic beauty territory. She reminded me a little bit of Audrey Hepburn, though her tastes ran more to dirty overalls and flip flops. Her hair was up in a high ponytail and there was dirt smudged on her cheeks. She was the total opposite of my other sister, Rose. I was somewhere in the middle. Average in most regards or so I thought.

"Hey, Ivy," she said as she leaned in to hug me. "Ooh, you smell good. Chamomile?" She pulled back and studied me. "You look tired. Everything okay?" Without waiting for me to answer, she rummaged around in the oversized bag on her shoulder and shoved a plant at me. "This is good for the air. It's a golden pothos. All you have to do is put it in a place with bright light and keep the soil moist."

I took it from her, eyeing the plant with trepidation. I liked plants - a lot, I just wasn't as good at keeping them alive as she was.

"I'm serious," she said, amusement filling her voice. "They're very easy." She clucked her tongue and stepped around me to come inside. "It's those orchids that stress you out," she chided as she walked over to the windowsill and perused my collection. I did have a weakness for orchids - even as temperamental as they were. But there was something so life-affirming about seeing those gorgeous blooms.

I watched as Holly touched one of the orchids I was having trouble with. Before my very eyes, the stem strengthened, the leaves grew brighter and several flower buds appeared on the stem.

"I wish I could do that," I murmured.

Holly laughed. "And I wish I could do what you do." She turned to face me. "You wouldn't happen to have any of that calming soap lying around, would you?"

I tilted my head in regard. "I do. Everything okay?"

A dark shadow crossed over her face and it was so surprising my mouth dropped open. I'd never seen Holly unhappy. Maybe when we were kids and emotions were running high. But she was the kind of person who let just about everything roll off her back. A second later, her happy expression was back. "Just fine!" she chirped. "I'm just burning the candle on both ends right now at work so I'm not sleeping all that well."

Her emotions were a maelstrom right now and she knew I knew it. Holly knew I could tell she was lying. A lot of people thought they had the ability to keep their emotions under control. This was somewhat true. People could hide their emotions from other people.

Not from someone like me.

My sister was upset and worried, tired and achy. I didn't sense any physical danger, but there was definite emotional danger. I wanted so badly to grill her about it, but we weren't kids anymore. I was twenty-six. My sister was twenty-four. Our other sister was twenty-eight. Too old to bully each other into spilling our secrets. I laid a hand across her arm. "I'll give you some of the calming soap, but I've been working on a new recipe if you want to try it. I can give you a couple of bars of it." A lot of people didn't like the way chamomile smelled, so I'd removed the herb and tried to formulate a new scent with lavender and sandalwood. Since sandalwood was considered a vulnerable plant, I tried not to overuse it. This particular batch was made for my own use. If it was successful, I'd have to secure a place with good environmental practices and make it in limited editions. It was for spiritual and mental relaxation. Not just for stress. Sometimes our spirit needed more rest than our physical bodies.

She gave me a warm smile. "I'd like that."

The sound of rattling footsteps made Holly's grin widen. Her eyes sparkled as she turned to the doorway only to see Harry clamber in wearing a bow tie and a top hat.

"Well!" she exclaimed. "Don't you look handsome!"

Harry's grinning visage stayed the same, but I could smell his happiness in the air. If it were possible for Harry to beam, I knew he would. The skeleton sketched an elaborate bow and tipped his hat to her.

"It's a pleasure to see you, Miss Bradshaw," he

said and stood a moment later, his eyes sockets beaming bright spirit blue.

"And how are you, fine sir?" she asked. Holly sounded genuinely pleased to see him and I was hard to fool. Those two had a weird dynamic I couldn't quite figure out, but if it made Holly happy to see Harry happy, who was I to stop them?

"My day has never been better now that you're here," Harry said, his crisp accent even sharper than usual.

"And mine the same," Holly returned graciously.

I rolled my eyes and headed into the kitchen. I'd let those two crazy kids catch up while I made some coffee.

2

Holly sat across from me, carefully mixing an exact amount of cream and sugar in her coffee. It always boggled my mind when I watched her do this. Who took exact amounts of those two things? My coffee was almost half milk and a teaspoon of sugar. Holly's was a disaster of milk and sugar. Sometimes it was only a little amount of each, sometimes her coffee was unrecognizable.

When she finished stirring and took a sip, she let out an audible sigh. "So good," she said to herself.

I always bought coffee directly from a farm overseas. Every six months I'd sit down and order enough to keep me stocked so I wouldn't have to worry if I ran out. Once my supply got down to about a month, I'd re-order. My sister wasn't that organized, so if her supply ever ran dry (which it did - often), she'd pop over here and rummage through mine.

"How's Rose?" she asked after a moment.

Rose and Holly didn't get along all that well. I was both the middle sister and trapped in the middle with those two. "She's doing well." I smiled at her knowing who she really wanted to know about. "The twins are wonderful. Ava and Archer start pre-school in a few weeks."

Her eyes glittered with wetness and sadness speared me in the heart. Holly refused to talk about what happened between her and Rose. I was doing an okay job at not interfering, but this wasn't Harry. This was about my sisters, so I wasn't sure how much longer I could pretend like nothing was wrong. "They ask about you," I said casually.

Holly took a shaky breath and set her mug down. She rummaged through her bag again and pulled out two gift-wrapped books. "Please give these to them." Holly gestured at the label. "They're different books. I tried to pick out what I thought they might like."

It had been six months since Holly last visited with the twins. I know her heart was breaking. She was the more sensitive of us. Rose was hard - or could be when she chose to. She was rigid and stalwart in her beliefs whereas Holly was morally flexible. It was the best way to describe her. I fell somewhere in the middle. I did my best to stick to my beliefs, but I also truly appreciated other people's thoughts and feelings about things. Holly was open to listening to anything and everything, and sometimes it felt like she formed opinions in a weird mishmash of other people's thoughts.

It drove Rose nuts.

But Rose drove Holly nuts with her rigidity. I didn't know what had gone wrong, but I knew this was a sticking point between them and, if I had to guess, I figured it probably had something to do with their silent argument. I took the packages. "Maybe one day you can give these to them yourself?" I suggested gently.

Holly's face went blank. "Perhaps not," she said, her voice measured and careful.

A sigh escaped me, but I nodded and set them on the coffee table. Rose would be over here in a couple of days anyway. Maybe I could sneak some pictures of the kids and send them to Holly. This all felt sort of like playing double agent in a spy comedy I didn't sign up for.

I loved them both. I could understand both sides.

But we were sisters and I wished they could get through this.

"I love you, Holly," I said instead.

She reached over and squeezed my fingers. "I love you, too."

We enjoyed our coffee then, mostly silent, but sometimes chattering about inane things. This was one of the things I loved about my sister. There was no judgment or disapproval. She just ... was.

I saw Harry peeking around the corner, no doubt trying to catch a glimpse of Holly. I rolled my eyes but didn't call him on it. When he saw me looking, he clicked off down the hall, his skull high and his shoulders unnaturally straight.

About an hour later, the door opened and my assistant, Piper, walked in. She waved at us. "So sorry to disturb you. I just popped in to drop off the new mica shipment. I didn't want to forget this tomorrow, so I figured I'd bring it in while I remembered." She held a box from Glam Micas - a company outside of Moonmist doing a brisk business in environmentally safe glitters and micas. I loved the company because of their sustainability but also because their micas were eye scorching bright. It made my soaps stand out against the competition. I might have magical soap, but I knew what caught the customer's eye. It had to be pretty, bright, and eye-catching. No one could see magic, but everyone could see magenta.

"Thanks, Piper!" I said and watched as she rounded the corner with the box.

I'd brought her on a few months ago when business was picking up so much I was having trouble getting my soap made. My supplies had run dangerously low and Piper had strolled into the shop as a customer. I'm not sure if she saw how frazzled I was or only saw an opportunity for work because she approached me and offered her service.

She was bright, cheery, pretty, and smart as a whip. I couldn't replace her if I tried.

So I vowed to never have to try.

My sister set her mug down and stood, groaning and stretching her way up. "It was good to see you." She reached over and pulled me into a tight hug. "Tell that bag of bones I said to be good. I'll see you soon."

I squeezed her before letting her go and walking her to the door. "I'll give your books to the twins."

She gave me a wobbly smile and waved when Harry came out to say goodbye. As soon as the door shut, my assistant came out with a strange look on her face.

"Everything okay?" I asked as I closed the door.

She pointed a thumb over her shoulder. "I was putting the mica away and decided to check the supplies out to make sure we had enough for the next few months. How many pounds of lye are we supposed to have?"

I walked back to the workroom with her. "I ordered a hundred pounds of lye last month," I told her as I opened up the lower cabinet. I was careful about where I kept the chemicals, but I didn't keep them locked up. I didn't have any children and my pup so far had no curiosity about my soaping supplies. I kept a close watch on her, but she was more interested in her squeaky dinosaur and her snack time than anything to do with my business.

"I thought so," she said and shook her head. Her brow was furrowed. "We're missing at least one box."

My head jerked up sharply. "Are you sure?"

She chewed the side of her lip. "Ninety-five percent. I'll have to get the receipts but if lye comes twenty pounds to a box and you've only used three boxes..." Her voice trailed off.

I pulled the boxes out and counted. "I'll be

darned," I whispered more to myself than anyone else. "But no one ever comes in here."

Piper shook her head. "We have people coming in and out of the shop constantly and we can't always watch everyone."

"But to take an entire box of lye out?" I scratched my chin and pondered how in the world it would be possible. "I guess a better question is why would they take it?"

"Another soap maker?" Piper asked, her thin shoulders raised in a shrug. "Seems odd."

I still wasn't convinced one of us hadn't misplaced it. Harry, who'd been hanging back, chimed in. "Before you ask, I have no need for lye. In fact, lye is detrimental to my kind."

I snorted. The skeleton had an addiction to true crime television, so thanks to him, I now knew lye was used by some clever criminals to get rid of bodies. When he told me I'd shuddered and refused to let him watch television for a week. Now he was more circumspect with the information he provided to me concerning facts about crime or unsolved murders.

"I figured you didn't take it," I told him. "But if you ever want to take up soaping, I could use an extra hand."

He made a noise of distress and clomped out of the room. Piper pressed her lips together to keep from laughing. "You really are hard on him sometimes."

I grinned at her. "He's way worse to me. I just remind him he's living rent-free in my house."

A chuckle escaped her before it died as she stared down at the lye. "Maybe we misplaced it," she said, though she didn't sound convinced.

"Maybe so," I agreed. It wouldn't be the first time either she or I had failed to put something in the right place. A large box of lye would be a little harder to lose, but it wasn't unheard of. There was no real need for an alarm right now. Not until we determined it wasn't misplaced. I stood up and wiped my hands on my soft jeans. "We'll figure it out."

Piper nodded. "Okay. I'll check my email to see if I can find the receipt. If not, it should be in the files. We'll figure it out."

She left after telling me where she'd put the mica. After she left, I went through all of the cabinets in the workshop to see if I'd accidentally put it somewhere else. When the search didn't provide any fruit, I left and went to the kitchen to clean up the mess Holly and I had made.

Harry came in just as I'd finished drying the last mug. Just like he always did. I'm sure the skeleton could hold a sponge or a broom, but he always made himself scarce any time chores were on the table.

"Did you find it?" he asked.

"The lye?" I asked as I put the mug in the cabinet.

"Yes. I wish I knew when it came up missing. It might help me remember who was in the store that day."

I glanced at him. "You remember who came into the store on any given day?" That would be some feat if he did.

He cleared his throat. "Of course I do," he said, not a modest note anywhere in his voice. "I'm not human, you know." He frowned as if he doubted that. "I'm a spirit, I think. So far, I'm immortal. Time doesn't run the same way it does for you."

I straightened. So perhaps he was way older than I thought he was. "Hmm," I said, "and how does time run for you exactly?"

Realizing his mistake, he stuttered for a bit before refusing to answer me. "Regardless of how old I am, time does run quite differently. If you can narrow down a day, I might be able to help you. If it's stolen," he said. "More likely you've lost it." The blue fire in his eyes shifted - Harry's version of an eye roll.

"Thank you," I told the skeleton. "Piper is tracking down the receipt to see when we ordered it. That should help narrow down the date some."

The doorbell rang and I left Harry in the kitchen. He wasn't a secret in the town - Moonmist was full of strange and wonderful things. Most people were fascinated by him. Some were repulsed. I tried not to get upset with those people - after all, when I first found out Harry was alive, I had a hard time accepting it or coming to terms with my new room-mate situation. However, I tried to make sure he made himself scarce during the times the shop was open. This shop was my livelihood. I'd never planned on an animate skeleton being part of my life.

"Hold on!" I called as I rushed over to open the door. Sam, the local librarian, stood outside holding a small stack of books.

"Ah! I exclaimed. "I almost forgot!" I shot him a grateful smile and reached for the books, ignoring how my heart skipped a beat at the sight of him. This had been going on for almost a year - ever since Sam had taken over for the other librarian. He'd been new to town and someone found out he was single. With the way every young female suddenly became interested in reading, I almost felt sorry for him. I'd stayed away - not wanting to add to the chaos - and tried to only go when I really needed something. We'd struck up a casual friendship, and I was careful not to ruin it. I didn't want to be one of the fawning sycophants throwing herself at him, and I think he was glad of it.

Sam was quietly handsome. A strong jaw, intelligent green eyes, and shaggy blond hair. He was taller than me, but less than six feet. If I had to guess maybe around five ten or so. His build was lean, almost like a swimmer, but there was coiled strength within him. When he spoke, it was deliberate. He never used ten words when five would do the same job.

"I couldn't find one of them," he said, his voice rumbly.

I flipped through them trying to remember everything I ordered.

"The one about trapping spirits." Sam scratched his chin. His eyes were curious, but he didn't ask any questions. I realized he didn't know about Harry. And ... I wondered why he'd stopped by with my books. Normally, he'd call and I'd swing by to pick them up.

I held the door open for him. "Come on in. I have something I want to show you."

Sam's eyebrows rose, but he stepped inside. I shut the door and called out for Harry. When he walked in, Sam's mouth dropped open.

"Say something, Harry," I said.

"Something Harry," the skeleton said.

Sam snorted with amusement and took a step closer. "My goodness." He walked around Harry, examining him from every angle. I couldn't stop the smile on my face. I didn't know what kind of magic Sam had, but I suspected it either had to do with books or intellect. Every new discovery made him almost childlike.

"Incredible," he murmured. "An animate skeleton." He scratched his head. "A spirit, perhaps?"

"Perhaps," Harry said, annoyance in his voice.

"You experience emotion?" Sam asked when he came around to stand beside me again.

Harry nodded, his grinning visage at odds with the tone of the question. "I'm just like a person but without all the pesky skin."

Sam looked at me. "He was the reason for the books?"

I nodded. "I'm trying to figure out why he can't leave the property." A laugh escaped me. "Actually, I'm trying to figure out what he is, how he was made and why he can't leave."

The quiet librarian examined Harry who appeared to squirm around under his scrutiny. "I'm invested in this," Sam said after a moment. "I'd like to help if you don't mind."

My eyebrows rose. I'd never turn down the chance to work with someone who had a mind like his. It didn't hurt that he was easy on the eyes. "Of course," I said at once. "I'd love that. You probably have more access to research material than I do, so I'll take all the help I can get."

He gave a sharp nod and turned to go. A smile hovered over my lips at his behavior. Sam wasn't socially awkward, exactly. More like social avoiding. We weren't the kind of friends to call each other every day, but I did know he didn't get out much. Gossip flew all over Moonmist, especially when Sam was attached to it.

I watched as he walked away without saying goodbye and just as he was about to walk down the steps, I cleared my throat. "Bye Sam."

He turned back around, his cheeks tinged pink. "Sorry," he said, embarrassment written all over him. "I forget sometimes."

I grinned at him. "It's okay. You brought me books so you're forgiven."

A smile made his left dimple peek out from his

cheek and made me a little weak-kneed. "See you later, Ivy," Sam said as he turned to go.

I waited until I closed the door to let out a dreamy sigh. Handsome. Smart. And worked in a library? Be still my beating heart. I knew nothing would ever come of my crush, but I still couldn't help it. I didn't get a lot of men in my soap shop and when they did come in, they were either searching for something for their wives or they knew what they needed before they ever stepped inside.

I carried a men's line, though all my soaps could be used by anyone. It was called Rugged. I made a line with fragrance oils such as Tobacco and another called Smoke and Whiskey, but I also had a line made with only essential oils. My favorite was made with Spruce and Sandalwood. It was both uplifting and mysterious. I had a bar I kept in my bathroom as a hand soap. If I couldn't have a boyfriend, I could at least smell like one occasionally.

"He's more into books than he is you," Harry said snidely.

I rolled my eyes and brushed past him. "Says the skeleton who's madly in love with my sister."

His jaw clicked shut. "Fair Ivy, you are a cruel mistress," he lamented as he followed me into the living room.

"You interested in a hunting trip?" I asked, ignoring his jibe. Harry couldn't resist the opportunity to go outside and forage around. Though he did less foraging and more talking than I did.

"I'll get my hat!" he declared. I shook my head and grabbed a light jacket and the basket I kept sitting right by the front door. I slid my feet into a pair of rain boots and waited for Harry. It was chilly these days in Moonmist, though the snow was still a while from arriving. Our temperatures were mild and controlled by several witches, one of them being my sister Rose. It was never too cold to be dangerous and never too hot to be scorching. Snow was allowed for only two weeks out of the year and it was always a guess as to when it would come. I didn't have to guess. Rose always told me. I knew for a fact we'd see snow in less than two weeks. I looked forward to it. I'd lived in other places other than Moonmist so I was used to not knowing when the seasons would switch or when it would be hot or cool. I loved the randomness of it and how it seemed like if you just waited a bit, the weather would change. But I also loved it here because I knew I would never be uncomfortable. Temperature control was a big draw for the paranormals and every day I saw new people in town. Moonmist Springs had always been an area full of vibrant, bustling little towns. I didn't know about the rest of the places, but the temperature in Tennessee could go from scorching to chilly and sometimes the weather was so humid, it felt like you were sitting in a sauna. I certainly didn't miss that.

Harry returned wearing a jaunty fedora which didn't make him look any less creepy. I held open the door and he clomped out, not bothering to take the basket from me. Harry was a lot of things, but he wasn't exactly a gentleman. Not to me anyway. Maybe because our relationship felt more like brother and sister than anything else.

I led Harry down to the woods behind my house. I had a lot of luck finding wildflowers and herbs in this area. Probably because of the two earth witches living on either side of me. Everything around their property seemed to grow a little larger and a little brighter. I was careful to stay only on my property when I gathered. Witches, no matter how nice they were, got a little weird when someone strayed onto their lands, even when it was by accident. Plus, I didn't want to trip any spells or anything. I didn't consider myself a witch - not exactly. I had magic, yes, but I didn't perform spells or make potions. Unless you counted bath oils or salts a potion. I didn't.

The weather was cool against my cheeks and the wind stirred my hair. I inhaled deeply, the scent of pine and crisp wind filling my body and easing my mind. I might not love the way I'd come to be here, but I loved Moonmist.

Harry was quiet beside me, the only sound the rattle of his bones as he walked. He loved going outside, but he wouldn't go without me. I didn't know why and when I asked, he wouldn't tell me. It didn't matter too much because occasionally he could be a big help. I'd taught him how to recognize certain plants and he would gather the ones I missed. Even though he had nothing resembling human eyes besides the sockets, he could still see far better than I could.

I took a small spade out of the basket and passed it over to Harry. I took the other for myself and knelt down at the beginning of the woods. A small patch of wild chamomile had sprouted up and I carefully dug up two of the plants while leaving the other two alone. I did my best never to take it all. Plants sprouted up all the time, but I didn't want to be responsible for taking the last of something even if it was on my property.

I lifted the plant up and smelled the cheery white flowers before I carefully placed it into the basket. Harry wandered off - not too far away - and I saw him kneel. I wasn't sure what he was gathering, but he knew what I needed so I didn't pay much mind. I walked and gathered for about half an hour before I heard Harry calling to me.

"Uh, Ivy?"

I straightened from my crouching position and winced as my back pulled in protest. I lifted the basket up and wandered over to where Harry was, his blue fedora visible through the dense tree cover. He stood looking down at something and the blue in his eye sockets was darker than usual.

He held a bony hand up. "Don't come any closer," he warned.

I stopped in my tracks and my eyes zoomed in to what he was looking at. At first, I didn't see anything unusual, but as I looked closer, I frowned. A pool of brown liquid puddled a few feet away. It was odd because it hadn't rained in several days, but it wasn't super unusual for there to be puddles of standing water around, especially in the woods.

Just as I opened my mouth to say something, my gaze caught a hint of bright white. I swallowed hard and looked back at the skeleton standing close to me. His bones were an aged yellowish color.

But I knew what bones looked like considering I'd been living with a pile of them for months now.

"Oh," I said faintly. "Is it an animal?"

"No," Harry said, his voice grim. "Definitely not an animal."

"I don't understand. I come out here at least once a week." I'd been over every part of these woods and had never seen this before.

"I think we found your missing lye," Harry said. He turned to face me.

Our gazes met. I frowned. "You can't possibly think -" I began.

"I don't have to think," Harry said, "I already know."

I dropped my basket and dug for my cell phone buried deep within my jacket pocket. As I dialed the number for emergency services, my head spun with the implications of this. When the dispatcher answered, I rattled off my location and what I found. When I hung up, I turned to Harry. "You're sure this is the result of lye?" My lips twisted as I stared down at the pool of liquid.

"Positive," he said. "I don't know why they didn't finish the job, though. Maybe they got in a hurry?" His bony shoulder rose and fell in a shrug. "Lye isn't something you should hurry with, but maybe they had to dispose of it before they planned to."

"Is there any way they can trace the lye?" I asked, my voice tremulous.

"Why Ivy," Harry said, his voice full of amusement, "are you trying to cover up a crime?"

I snorted, but my voice was tremulous. "If this was my lye, I'm not sure what to think," I admitted. "Why would someone go to all that trouble?"

"I wouldn't worry too much. Lye is a common purchase. They might be able to tell what lye it is, but it's doubtful. Sodium hydroxide is just that - sodium hydroxide. I don't know if the formulation ever wavers."

But I had been missing at least one box of it before finding this today. A shiver ran down my spine. Why had mine been taken? It wasn't exactly a crime of opportunity. The shop is too busy and was staffed all the time. Plus I lived where I worked.

I scratched my chin before I moved several feet away and plopped in the grass. I motioned for him to head home. "Humans sometimes work on the police force," I told him. "It might be best if you were to go back to the house."

Harry gasped, affronted. He liked to be right in

the midst of drama and gossip. I rolled my eyes. "I'll tell you everything," I said. "I promise."

He harrumphed as he slowly made his way out of the woods. "You'd better, Ivy. You don't know what it's like being a pile of bones."

I'm sure I didn't. I scooted a little further back from the bones and waited for the police to show up.

3

There wasn't a whole lot of need for a police force in Moonmist because magic workers usually policed themselves, so they tended to work with a skeleton crew. Around here that could be taken literally, especially with Harry in the picture, but they were mostly human. I suspected the Police Chief was a magic user, but the officers were either low in magic or human. However, when the cruiser pulled up, I could sense magic beating off one of them. I'd never seen him before so he must be new to the area.

The first one was a man named Carey. He was friendly and upbeat every time I saw him, and he had every reason to be. He'd married a pretty little witch named Suzie, and she'd just given birth to a little darling daughter. I stood, brushing damp leaves from the set of my pants. "Hey!" I called, waving to Carey.

His face brightened in a smile but dimmed when he remembered why he was here. The other man gave off an odd air. He was powerful. Any magic-user could see that. But he also seemed ... dangerous. I stifled my shudder and gave him a polite nod. "Hello."

He returned my nod, but he didn't smile, nor did he meet my eyes. Instead, his gaze roamed around the property and everywhere else before it landed where the bones were. Without waiting for me to say something, he walked right over to them and stared down, lifting his hands in the air.

My brow furrowed as I watched.

"Necromancer," murmured Carey, so low I could barely hear him.

My eyebrows shot up to my hairline. I'd never met one. "Really?" I asked, trying not to sound too excited. "Does Moonmist have any of those?"

Carey pointed. "We do now. It took a lot of bargaining to get him on the force with us. One of the other towns tried to snatch him from right under our noses, but we ended up winning him in the end." Carey stood straighter, a proud look on his face. I chewed my lip to keep from smiling. It was weird to be happy you'd essentially "won" someone. I bet they were paying him a bundle. Necromancers were worth their weight in gold. Most of them set up shop and charged a mint to talk to deceased relatives. My initial estimation of him went up a notch because he'd chosen the police force instead.

I watched as a trickle of green magic flowed from him to the ground. Seconds later, he shook his head and turned back to us.

"Male," he said, his voice a low attractive rumble. Dark hair rustled in the wind and gave him a rakish air. His eyes were light - the color of brown sugar. A sharp jawline and a straight nose gave him the look of a model rather than a peacekeeper. His attractive-ness was marred only by a large scar that graced his left cheek. I didn't know what had done that, but it was difficult to scar a magic-user. We were constantly expending energy and research showed our cell turnover was much faster than a human's. I wonder what the wound had looked like when it happened.

"Miss?" The man said, his tone annoyed. He'd caught me looking at his scar.

"Um, Ivy," I said. My name is Ivy Bradshaw. I own

the property right there." I hooked a thumb over my shoulder.

One of his eyebrows rose. "I asked when you found this."

Color flooded my cheeks. "Oh." I wished the earth would open and swallow me whole. "Less than fifteen minutes ago."

Was that amusement in his eyes? But as soon as I saw it, it flickered away making me wonder if I imagined it. I was an idiot. I pointed to my basket. "I come out here twice a week and gather plants for my soaps. This is the first time I've seen it," I babbled. "What is it, do you think? Human?"

Carey cleared his throat. "No idea," he interjected. "Forensics is on its way out. They can tell us more once they've had the chance to analyze it."

"It's definitely human," the handsome officer said. "Male. Between the ages of 30-35."

Necromancy was cool. So cool. "You can tell all that with just ..." I wiggled my fingers around.

He snorted, though it sounded more derisive than amused. "I can," he acknowledged.

His name tag read Kramer. He probably had a cool first name like Rock or Heath or something. But Officer Handsome here didn't seem like he was terribly nice. I turned back to Carey, turning my back to Officer Handsome. "Tell me what you need from me." I pointed to my basket. "I need to get these inside and dry them soon."

Carey's gaze lingered on Kramer before they slid back to me. "Just tell me what you were doing and how you came across it. I'm sure we'll have more questions later, but we can start with that."

I told him everything I knew, leaving out the presence of Harry. I don't think Carey knew I had an animate skeleton living with me, so I wasn't going to try to explain that. I wanted them gone so I could get inside and finish my work for the day. The sun had long since set on Moonmist, but the town was never truly dark here. The weather workers controlled the temperature, but they also controlled the atmosphere. We were very much like Alaska. Sometimes it was dark, but for most of the year, the town only experienced dusk. Even when it was nighttime, the moon was usually bright enough to read a book by.

When Carey finished asking questions, he clicked his pen off and tucked his notepad back into his pocket. "Thanks, Ivy. I'll be in touch if we need anything else from you."

My eyes lingered on the bones. "Do I need to do anything with that?"

"Absolutely not," Kramer interjected. "Touching it could be considered tampering with evidence." His voice was almost an angry bark. I flinched.

A quick flash of anger showed on Carey's kind face. I took a step back. He held a hand up. "She was only asking to be nice, Kramer. Relax, would you?"

Kramer's face darkened, but he turned away before I could really sense what he was thinking. Embarrassment flooded off of him and I quickly dulled my senses so it wouldn't overwhelm me. He was also experiencing ... grief. That was odd, especially since he said he couldn't tell who it was. Empathy rang within me, even though I didn't care much for Officer Kramer.

"It's okay," I said when the silence had stretched on for too long. "I'll just head back inside."

"Try to stay out of the area for a few days at least," Carey said, his tone much kinder than Kramer's had been.

I nodded. "That won't be a problem." I tilted my head back to the house. "If you want to come on up to the shop, I'll grab your wife some of that soap she likes. I haven't given you two a baby gift yet, and I have some bars of a new gentle Castile blend soap she might like." I gave him a gentle smile. "It might help the baby sleep a little better."

His eyes lit up and I led him and Officer Kramer back to my house. I didn't even have to use my magic to tell how exhausted Carey was. I could see it in the dark circles under his eyes. But I could also tell when he stood beside me by the slump of his shoulders and his weary posture. I couldn't imagine how his poor wife was feeling.

Once inside, I led Carey over to the workshop and packed him up some of the Raspberry Vanilla Serenity bars and three of the new baby soap formulations I'd come up with. I hadn't named it yet, but I'd used Lavender, German Chamomile and a hint of Mandarin oil in the blend. The soap was only made with those essential oils, olive oil, and lye. It had been curing for twelve full months because of how soft olive oil only soap was. I'd tried it on myself in the shower just last week and had fallen in love with it, but I didn't have enough to stock it full time in the store. These bars were precious, but I liked Carey and I liked his wife. They deserved to be well-rested. I wrapped the bars in parchment paper and put them in a small bag. "This should help," I told him. "Just be careful to keep it out of the baby's eyes. It's gentle soap, but it's still soap."

"Thanks so much, Ivy," he said, the relief palpable in his eyes.

I patted his arm. Kramer stood beside him, his massive arms crossed over his chest. I didn't want to give him anything at all, but I had something I thought could help him. I let my gaze linger on him for a moment while I thought. Bending down, I opened up the bottom cabinet and pulled out a soap I didn't sell too often. It was one of my favorites, but only heavy magic users favored it. I'd called it Restless Soul and only set it out when I had a feeling someone would come in who might need it. This one took months of trial and error before I'd perfected it. I wanted something to appeal to both sexes and many of the oils traditionally used for grief were florals. I'd finally nailed the combination of Rose, Sandalwood, Patchouli, and Ylang Ylang. The end result was a heady, mysterious mix of floral and woodsy scents along with a hefty dose of feel-good magic. I wrapped up the bar and handed it to Kramer.

He hesitated before taking it.

"For you," I told him. "Try it before you knock it. You might like it."

From the look on his face, he didn't agree with me. I refrained from rolling my eyes. A good bar of soap was a good bar of soap. He didn't have to like me to like the bar. But if he did like it, I might be able to score another customer. Though it would prob-ably be online sales. Kramer didn't seem like the kind of guy who'd come into a soap shop and browse for himself. I could be wrong, but I didn't think so. He was probably the kind of guy who hated every-thing about shopping malls and only ate steak for protein.

He eyed the bar of soap like it was about to bite him.

"Relax," Carey told him for the second time. "Her soaps are magic. That's why she's the only soaper in this town. No one else can compete with Ivy."

My smile was genuine this time. Carey didn't know how true his words were. Others couldn't compete with me because no one else had the kind of magic I did. Until someone else came along like me, I had total job security.

After I escorted both of the officers out, I collapsed on my couch and groaned. What a weird day this was. Harry poked his head out a couple of minutes after hearing the door closed. "How'd it go?" he asked as he settled himself into my old, soft recliner.

"There's a new police officer in Moonmist." I paused for dramatic effect, knowing how much

Harry lived for idle gossip. When I heard the impatient shifting, I smiled. "He's a necromancer."

Harry's gasp told me it was worth it. "A necromancer?" he repeated in awe. "He's the first one of those in this town, isn't he?"

I nodded. "I think so. He was able to tell the bones were male and his age. Somewhere around 30-35 years old."

"Hmm," Harry said. When he spoke next, his voice was hesitant. "Do you think ..." He stopped.

I turned to look at him. "Think what?"

"Do you think he could help me?"

I stilled as I thought about it. Helping Harry hadn't come to mind when I found out about Kramer's magic. "I don't know," I said honestly. "Those might not be your bones, so I don't think he'd be able to tell much about you."

"But I'm dead," Harry said. "I think."

"Maybe," I acknowledged. "Maybe not. We know you're a spirit, but there are a lot of spirits out there. It doesn't necessarily mean you're human."

Harry grunted. "I'm probably human," he mumbled.

My eyebrows rose. I waited to see if he would elaborate.

"As I age, memories come back to me," he admitted. "I think I might be human. Will you pose the question to him next time you see him?"

My lips twisted at the thought of Kramer being around more often. He was handsome, but he didn't seem all that nice. And yet ... how could I say no to Harry? "I'll see what he says."

A breath escaped Harry and I had to chuckle. If I didn't know he was a pile of bones, I would have suspected him to be a living, breathing person. "Thank you, Ivy."

"My pleasure," I told the skeleton.

The doorbell rang then and I groaned at the thought of having to get up. I'd had a busy day and had almost forgotten about Lacey coming home. Even as I didn't want to move, I also wanted to snuggle with the bundle of energy that was my new lab pup. I opened the door and immediately locked my knees to steady myself. Lacey launched herself at me, making me sway on my feet. I'd learned a long time ago how strong she was and how quickly she could knock me over in her excitement. I bent down to scratch her behind the ears and Lacey immediately fell over onto her back for a belly rub. I snickered and obliged her.

The dog trainer, Charlie, stood there, smiling fondly at Lacey.

"How'd she do today?" I asked as Lacey wiggled happily.

"Good, Ms. Bradshaw." Charlie handed over the leash to me. "She's still full of puppy energy and struggles with impulse control, but we're working on that." He handed me over a folder. "These are the things to be working on with her. I'll come back tomorrow afternoon and pick her up."

I shot him a grateful smile. "Thanks so much. We're still working on potty training, but she hasn't had an accident in two weeks. How'd she do at your house?"

Charlie's smile widened. "Perfect. This little girl went straight to the door and scratched once. I think you're safely on your way to saying she's officially potty trained."

I exclaimed what a good girl Lacey was and wished Charlie a good night. He waved and jogged back down the stairs. I rubbed Lacey's belly for a few more seconds and got up to close the door. "Come on, girl," I said and led her through the house to the back, just in case. She was an eight-month-old Lab mix and I'd gotten her through a series of comical accidents. I loved her to pieces, but she could be a challenge sometimes. The trainer assured me a tired dog was a happy dog, so I did my best to keep her as active as I could manage. She still had about four more weeks of three times a week training before she'd graduate her doggy class. So far, it had been worth every penny.

Lacey sat down at the door and waited for me to open it. "Good girl," I said and gave her another pat. As soon as I opened the door, she jogged out, looked behind her and, once reassured, she ventured out to do her business. Lacey tended not to go very far without me and that was a good thing. She was so fast I wouldn't even dream of being able to catch her if she decided to dart away. She was a bit of a scaredy-cat, too, which worked in my favor.

Once we were inside, I locked up all the doors and ventured into the kitchen to make a hot chocolate. Lacey watched me the entire time and I had to chuckle. "You can't have any of this, little girl. Chocolate is bad for pups." I grimaced down at the hot chocolate I'd just added a massive dollop of whipped cream to. "It's bad for me, too," I muttered, even as I took it back to the living room and flipped on the television. Lacey hopped up and laid her head on my lap. Some people didn't want their dogs on the couch. I figured I had no kids and no other companion besides a skeleton, so if Lacey wanted to be on the couch, I'd let her.

She was a good dog and a good companion for me, even if she thought I was a weird human sometimes. I had some trouble interpreting Lacey's moods, but I was getting better at it. Right now, she was tired and content.

Even though the day had ended a little strange and scary, I had to admit I felt the same as Lacey.

4

———

I was up at the crack of dawn thanks to an active puppy and being unable to stop thinking about the bones on my property. Lacey wriggled and barked at me as I walked to the back door like a zombie. She flew outside, and I headed right over to the coffee pot.

Two hours later, I flipped my shop sign to *Open* and was working on my third cup of coffee. The bell over the door jingled less than five minutes after I opened up shop. To my surprise, Officer Handsome aka Kramer stood there.

He wore a strange expression as he glanced around. When his gaze fell on me, he schooled his expression into blankness.

"Good morning, Officer Kramer," I said politely. I

slid out of my seat and walked over to him. "Is this about soap or yesterday?"

He cleared his throat, obviously uncomfortable. "I'd like to purchase some more of your soap," he said quietly.

Inside, I wanted to whoop with joy. He must have used it last night. "The bar I gave you will last at least three weeks," I said. "I just wanted to make sure you knew that before I sold you any more."

Kramer nodded. "I don't want to run out." He shifted and scratched the back of his neck. "It was ..." A breath escaped him.

Empathy filled me. Certain types of magic - like mine - didn't take a lot out of the user. My magic was uplifting usually, bright and happy. Granted, it wasn't always like that simply because I could feel people's emotions. Right now Kramer was confused and in disbelief. But he was also relieved, and I could sense hope within him. Magic like his was darker. It took more from the user. I suspected the soap would work for him even though we had no necromancers around here. But we did have a lot of people who worked with grief and trauma, and those people were repeat customers. I didn't know a whole lot about necromancy, but I knew it involved working with grieving loved ones and occasionally law enforcement.

I reached over, hesitant at first, and laid a hand on his arm. "It's okay. I understand. How many bars would you like? Soap has a long shelf life, but it does take a while to cure. So I can sell you what I have, but I'll have to make more right away. I think two more bars would hold you for quite a while." I tapped my finger on my chin and thought about the other customers I had who used the blend. "But I'd like to keep four bars back for other customers."

He blinked at me. "Two would be fine, Miss Bradshaw." Lacey walked in just then, her collar jingling. She looked like a shadow moving through the store.

Kramer's face cleared and a wide smile appeared on his face. The effect of it was like standing in the sun after months of darkness. My heartbeat picked up as he bent down to scratch Lacey behind the ears.

My traitorous dog scooted close and leaned her entire body against his knees. He chuckled and picked her up. Lacey's tongue lolled out of her mouth as he held her like a baby.

Every single judgment I'd had against Kramer fell out of my head at that moment. He loved dogs and he wasn't too uptight to admit when he was wrong.

"Lab mix?" he inquired.

I nodded dumbly. Handsome and liked dogs? Toast. I was toast.

"Where did you get her?"

Lacey reached up to try to lick Officer Handsome in the face. Gah. The cuteness. "I found her wandering down the street and picked her up to take her to the shelter so they could try to find her owner. I found her on my front porch a few hours later, so I took her back." The memory made me laugh. "The second time she showed up on my porch the same day, I took it as a sign from the universe."

"That's because she's a very good girl, aren't you?"

Lacey couldn't be any happier than if someone filled a baby pool full of hot dogs and let her swim in it.

"I'll um go fill your soap order," I said and went to the back before he could say anything. Was I in the Twilight Zone? I didn't want to like him, but it was hard to resist a man in uniform who also scooped my pup up and cooed to her like she was a baby. I shook my head as I wrapped up two more bars of the Restless Soul soap. When I came back out, there were two more customers in the shop, so I handed over the bag and told him it was on the house.

"Oh I couldn't," he protested.

"You can. But next time I expect payment," I said, a teasing note in my voice. "I'm just glad I could help you. Since you're a new customer and new to Moonmist, please accept it as a welcome gift."

He stared down at the package, indecision written in every line of his body.

"Truly," I assured him. Our gazes met. "Welcome to Moonmist."

Officer Kramer swallowed hard and nodded. "Thank you, Miss Bradshaw."

"Ivy, please," I said. "I'll make another batch this week. It takes at least six weeks to cure, but I like to go eight to make sure the bar is hardened enough."

He nodded. "This is really nice, Miss -" He laughed. "Ivy. Thank you for your kindness." Officer Kramer turned to go but he stilled. "Sloane," he said.

"Sloane?" My brow furrowed.

"My name," he said and chuckled, a deep, low rumble in his chest. "Sloane Kramer."

"Ah," I said. "It's nice to meet you, Sloane Kramer."

"Likewise," he said and turned to leave.

I watched Sloane until I couldn't see him

anymore. It just goes to show you can never really know anyone until you're around them for a while. I still didn't feel like I knew him, but I knew him a little better now and sometimes that was just as good.

CUSTOMERS FLITTED in and out for the better part of the day and when six p.m. rolled around, I flipped the sign to *Closed.* The trainer had stopped by to pick Lacey up around four, so I still had a couple of hours of free time. I yelled goodbye to Harry and headed out the door.

Moonmist was a beautiful town. Pine trees were prevalent here and I inhaled deeply every time I stepped outside. The air always had a crisp, clean tang to it. The wind gently ruffled my hair. I didn't bother driving to town and thought for the hundredth time I should sell my car. I could walk to town in less than five minutes. Since downtown was where everything important was, there was really no need for me to keep it. I'd used it maybe once since I'd arrived. I could get my lye shipped to my house for a pretty low price if I ordered enough of it, so I had no real reason to keep the vehicle anymore.

I waved at the pretty witch raking leaves in the yard next to mine.

She gave me a bright smile and a wave. "Hey Ivy!" she called. Luna was an earth witch and from the state of her front landscape - a talented one. Flowers in every color bloomed riotously and ivy tipped with gorgeous purple flowers crawled up the side of her house. Her grass was so bright green it almost looked fake. Even the leaves she was raking were brighter than the ones in my yard. I envied her powers, but I also wasn't jealous. If my yard got too bad, I could barter with Luna for a yard touch up. She couldn't resist my chocolate chip cookies.

Downtown bustled with residents, all of them busy running errands or shopping for pleasure. I stopped by the Yarn Wizard first. As soon as I opened the door, the owner rushed over to me. "Ivy!" she said, a huge smile on her face. "I got that yarn in you've been asking for." She waved at me to follow her and I dutifully let her lead the way.

Marsha was a staple in Moonmist. She'd been here for as long as I could remember and when I returned home after being gone so long, she was still here and running the shop. She was tiny - compact and lean, but I'd long ago lost track of how old she actually was. By my last count, she was somewhere in her 80's. Marsha zipped along through the store with a speed belying her age until she stopped behind the register and pulled a massive box onto the counter.

I started to protest her lifting it by herself but she waved me away. "The day I can't lift a box of yarn is the day I retire from this business," she groused at me.

I stepped away and let Marsha handle it. She opened the box and pulled out a beautiful blue-gray soft yarn. "Oh," I exclaimed. I was a new knitter and almost felt guilty about buying this yarn because I didn't want to mess it up. "This is gorgeous."

Marsha nodded. "You sure you know how to use it?" I hid a smile. Yarn wasn't a car, but the die-hards didn't like some of the newbies coming in and wasting their yarn. I lovingly referred to them as the "Yarn Mafia".

I nodded. I wouldn't tell her even if I didn't. "This is wonderful." I reached down for my purse. "How much do I owe you?"

Marsha rang it up and when she finished, she gave me a speculative look. "I heard the police found something interesting on your property yesterday." Her tone was casual but her eyes were eagle sharp. I wondered when this would happen. There wasn't much that could be hidden from the residents of Moonmist. I didn't like to participate in their gossip games, but I did like being kept informed sometimes. I threw her a small morsel of gossip.

"Yes," I shuddered, making it worse for Marsha's benefit. "Can you believe it? A pile of bones on my property."

"How horrible," Marsha said, eating the gossip up. "Do they know who it was?"

I refrained from telling her about Sloane's opinion. I'm sure he wouldn't appreciate me spreading information about the case. "They don't," I told her, making false regret seep into my voice. "I'm sure they'll find out soon." With the way information leaked around her, I'm sure she'd know before I did. "The whole thing was so shocking."

Marsha's eyes were full of avarice. "I'm sure, Ivy." She reached over to pat my hand. "So," she began, "I guess they think it's ..." her voice lowered. "Murder?"

I touched my chest in surprise. "Murder? I don't know about that." I hid my smile. Of course it was murder. I couldn't imagine jumping into a lye pit and dumping myself out in someone else's property. She was fishing for more information.

"You don't happen to know anyone who's setting up shop around here, do you?" I asked innocently.

Marsha bagged my yarn and printed out the receipt. "What do you mean by setting up shop?"

The comment about a soap competitor kept playing in the back of my mind. Someone like that would be buying lye. A lot of it. "Someone making soap," I said.

"Oh," Marsha drawled knowingly. "You trying to check out your competition?"

I gave her a tight smile. "Something like that," I assured her.

Her lips twisted to the side and she looked over her shoulder to make sure no one was listening. Her voice dropped to a low murmur. "You didn't hear this from me, but I overheard someone down at the ice cream shop talking about someone asking around about a storefront around here. Someone new in town. I can't remember her name. Tristi or Trin or -"

"Trinity?" I asked, my blood running cold. If it was Trinity I was going to run screaming out of this shop. I hadn't seen her in over ten years, but we had a longstanding rivalry. She always tried to copy me even though our magic was completely different. The day I left Moonmist, I breathed a sigh of relief I wouldn't have to deal with her anymore.

Marsha snapped her fingers. "That's her name!"

Her gaze turned cagey. "She was asking an awful lot of questions about you."

I shrugged. "I wouldn't know why." I knew exactly why. Trinity Blackwood was the kind of person who couldn't let anyone else have something better than her. If you had it and she wanted it, she'd do her best to get it, even if it meant doing something horrible to have it.

She used to be my best friend. I blinked away the memory and picked up the bag. "Thank, Marsha," I said as I turned to go.

"Wait!" Marsha cried.

My shoulders stiffened, but I couldn't alienate one of the best gossip sources in the entire town.

"Do you know when they're going to be able to identify who it was in your yard?" Marsha's voice was low and breathy. Annoyance washed over me. This was one of the lesser-known evils of living in a small town.

"I don't," I said, my voice a notch cooler than it had been a moment before. "I'm sure they won't tell me, though. The remains might be on my property, but they don't have anything to do with me."

"Hmm," Marsha said, but her focus was no longer on me. "I wonder where I can find out..." Her voice trailed off and I whisked myself out the door before she could catch me again. As soon as I stepped outside, I exhaled a deep, steadying breath. Marsha wasn't a bad person, but her energy was too much. She was constantly seeking, greedy for any hint of information she didn't know. It made trying to have a conversation with her exhausting.

I was just about to open my car door when I saw the familiar shaggy head of Sam, the librarian. He headed my way and held his hand up in greeting.

"Miss Bradshaw!" he called.

"Ivy," I reminded him for no less than the tenth time. His gaze flicked to mine.

"Ivy. Right. Sorry." He shook his head, his amber eyes glinting with annoyance at himself. "Listen, I went back to the library and I found a couple of things that might help answer your questions. Mind if I drop them by later?"

I blinked in surprise. "That was fast."

His expression was expectant.

"Oh. Yes," I said. "Of course. I'll be home in about an hour and a half if you want to swing by then?"

Sam nodded. "Sounds good. Take care, Ivy."

I finished up my errands, suddenly not minding at all that Trinity Blackwood had somehow managed to get into my head again.

5

The doorbell rang almost right on the dot an hour and a half later. I'd gotten home twenty minutes prior and changed into a pair of leggings and a long off-shoulder tunic top. It was chilly inside the house, so I pulled on a pair of chunky socks. The pot of decaf I'd just made finished brewing and I was pouring myself a cup when I heard someone step onto the porch.

"Coming!" I called at the sound of the bell.

Sam stood there, wearing his usual attire of flannel and jeans. I motioned for him to come in and he hesitated before stepping inside.

"I have a pot of decaf," I called as I walked back to the kitchen. "You want a cup?"

The heavy fall of his steps sounded as he followed behind. "I'd love one."

Once I finished making my cup, I poured one for him. "Cream or sugar?"

"A little cream, please." Sam pulled a barstool out and sat. He laid a canvas bag full of books on top of the counter and started pulling them out.

I pushed his mug over and eyed the titles. "*Spirituality in Utero*?" I grimaced and met his gaze.

A huff of laughter came from him. "Just trust me. I know that one seems weird, but there's some good information in there."

I let my eyes widen comically. "If you say so."

Sam's grin made the edges of his eyes crinkle, giving him a very Robert Redford look. Smart and handsome. No wonder he had women beating down his door. I pulled the rest of the books over. "*The Adventurer's Guide to Necromancy*." That one got a laugh out of me. Then, "*Binding Spirits as Servants: The Magician's Guide to Servitude*." My fingers fell away from that book. "Yuck," I said.

"Definitely," Sam agreed, "but it has the most information I'd found so far, so we might have to put our bias aside for a while. At least until we can rule it out."

There was an odd tingle from the book. Unpleasant, but not wicked. Not quite. It was grey magic. Odd with the title of the book being about servitude. "I'll reserve judgment. For now," I added tartly.

Sam snorted. "We'll start with that one and go through the others. Is Harry here?"

There was a slight tinge of excitement to his voice when he asked. Sam was, at heart, an intellectual, and Harry presented a confounding mystery to him. He was caught firmly between magic and science. After all, it wasn't so long ago when unexplainable things were considered witchcraft and now fell square into the science category.

But when I looked at Harry and when I talked to him, I knew there was darker magic afoot than him being merely trapped. We didn't have to figure it out right now, but we would figure it out. Eventually.

"Harry!" I called.

The skeleton clomped into the room a few moments later. His blue eyes flared brighter when he saw what Sam had brought with him. "Do you think these will help me discover ..." he paused. "What I am?"

Sam nodded. "I hope so. I haven't had the time to read through all of them, but I did find some promising passages. It would help if I could sit and talk with you. If I could ask you some specific questions, it would help me narrow down what magic was used to trap you."

If a skeleton could stiffen, that's what Harry did. There was a long pause before he answered. "I'd rather keep my past - what I can remember - to myself if you don't mind."

Silence fell in the room. Sam was the first to speak. "Okay, Harry." He held up his hands in surrender. "I didn't mean to pry. I just thought it would help me find the answers faster. No harm done."

Harry gave him a short nod and walked out of the room.

Sam's eyebrows raised as his gaze met mine. "Is he like that all the time?"

I slowly shook my head. "He's never forthcoming with information about himself, but I've never seen him clam up quite like that."

"Hmmm," Sam mused. His eyes went back to the hallway Harry had disappeared in. "I'll keep looking for a little while, but if he doesn't want to help, this might come to a standstill."

I frowned down at the books. "How much longer do we have to go?"

Sam laughed, a deep rolling chuckle. "This is what librarians thrive on. A mere mortal could not compete with how long we can sit in one position reading."

"Pizza?" I asked, pulling my cell phone out of the side pocket of my leggings.

He gave me a surprised look. "Err."

"Just pizza," I drawled. "Don't worry. I won't kidnap you and take you home to meet my mother."

Sam laughed, though there was definite relief in there. I grinned at him and decided to ask the question I'd been dying to for a while.

"How do you put up with it?" I asked as I opened up the app to order pizza. "Also, pizza preference?" I bowed my head as I perused the pizza offerings.

"With the women?" Sam asked, knowing the answer.

"Yep. Your Moonmist harem."

A surprised laugh burst from Sam. "I'm not sure I'd go that far," he said, his voice amused. He cracked open the servitude book and pulled a bookmark from it. Color bloomed on his cheeks. "It's all very innocent."

"I'm not saying it isn't," I said as I added a pepperoni, black olive, and mushroom pizza to my cart. "But do you ever get tired of it?"

Sam sighed. "I've been tired of it for a while."

"Hmm," I said.

"Also, add a pepperoni with black olives and mushrooms and I'll split it with you and pay for the extra toppings."

My fingers stilled over the keys. "I already did."

Sam scoffed. "Fibber."

I held my phone out to show him. "Oh ye of little faith. Who knew, Librarian? We're kindred pizza souls."

He scanned my phone with his gaze and when he looked at me again, there was something ... different in his eyes.

I dropped my gaze and added garlic bread knots in for good measure. After I ordered, I sipped my coffee and studied his profile. "You know they have a betting pool for who's going to crack the great Sam Carroll." I paused for effect. "I bet $20 on Maggie Thorne."

Sam laughed again. "The candle witch?"

I snorted delicately. "She's not a candle witch. She works with fire. Candles are a way for her to channel that energy. Fire is a dangerous talent to have." I slid him a side-eye. "She's very pretty."

"You're going to lose your $20," Sam retorted.

I laughed. "Alright, let's get down to business." As much as I enjoyed bantering with him, Lacey would be home in a little while and I didn't want to be up too late.

"One more thing," Sam said. His gaze turned serious. "What happened out here yesterday?"

"Ah, you heard already?"

"This is Moonmist," Sam said dryly. "Everyone heard."

"I'm not sure," I told him. "Harry was the one to find him. It's very weird to think those bones were an actual body." I shuddered.

"Someone said something about liquid?" Sam wasn't the type to gossip idly. He wanted to know for research purposes.

I nodded, not seeing the harm in telling him. "Some kind of liquid. I'm not sure what it was." I wouldn't tell him Harry strongly suspected it was lye. "It was almost like they dissolved it. Or tried to." I shrugged. "I don't really know. I suspect they'll know who it was in a day or so. Then they can try to figure out what happened."

"But why was it dumped on your property?"

The same thing bothered me. "No idea. The entire thing is really weird."

"There aren't a lot of things that can dissolve a body," he mused. "Lye is one of them." He glanced around. "Which you probably have a lot of."

There was no accusing note in his voice which was nice. I didn't think I could handle it if he thought I was somehow responsible. However, in the back of my mind niggled a tiny shred of doubt about my missing lye. It seemed too much of a coincidence for lye to be used in a crime and a body to be found in a soap maker's backyard.

I didn't believe all that much in coincidence. "I do," I admitted. "It's a main soap ingredient. But I can assure you, I've never tried to dissolve a body using lye. I much prefer to use my powers for good and not evil."

"Good," Sam said and pushed the book closer to me. He pointed out a passage. "This says witches used to curse humans by indenturing them in objects for crimes they didn't feel could be properly punished by the authorities." His finger hovered over the crimes. "Murder, Adultery, Harm to a child or livestock."

My lips twitched. "I'm not sure children and livestock are quite in the same category but I get what they're saying. So you think it might be a punishment for something he did in a past life?"

"Very possible," Sam said. "I'm leaning even more that way because of his refusal to speak with me. Since he's pretty tight-lipped with you too, I can only imagine it's something he might feel deep regret over."

I eyed the door and thought about it. Harry had never raised a bony hand in my direction. I didn't think he could do a lot of damage in his present form, but I did know he had some magic. He just preferred not to use it. The one time he had, I'd been astonished at his power.

"I'll try to work on him to see if we can figure it out. I'm more interested in the power required to perform a spell like that and to be able to maintain it for so long."

"If it's a curse, there's no focus," Sam murmured, his attention pulled to the next book.

My eyes widened. "There's no object or circle holding the spell steady?"

"Not with a curse. Those are usually tied to bloodlines. Breaking the spell breaks the curse, but if we don't know what curse it is, we don't know how to break it."

"I feel like that's warmer than I've ever been with trying to figure this out. And it fits." I beamed at him just as the doorbell rang.

I paid the pizza guy and dished us up some pizza. Just as I was about to sit down, Lacey made it home - a wriggling bundle of energy. By the time I got her settled down, my pizza was lukewarm and Sam was standing up.

A sting of disappointment went through me as I realized he was leaving, but I smiled and thanked him. "The pleasure was all mine," he said as he pulled some bills out of his wallet and dropped them on the table. "Thanks for the pizza." He reached down and scratched Lacey behind the ear. Her tongue lolled out as she gave him a doggy grin. Sam laughed and let himself out.

I stared down at Lacey. "You get all the boys," I said.

6

———

$\mathcal{M}$y sister, Rose, showed up on my doorstep the next morning. Normally when I saw my sister, she was frazzled and trying to wrangle the twins. By the time her visits were over, I was just as frazzled as she was. Today she was by herself. Rose gathered her gray cardigan around her spare frame and glared at me when I peeked out the window.

"Like you have visitors outside of business hours," she growled. "Open the door! It's cold out here."

Just for that, I went a little slower. When the door opened, Rose brushed inside without an invite. She rubbed her arms and shivered. "It feels colder than usual."

I shut the door behind her. "You would know, wouldn't you?"

Rose was one of the Moonmist Weather witches - one of five who worked tirelessly to keep the atmosphere temperate. She rolled her eyes at this and headed right to my kitchen to get a cup of coffee. All the Bradshaw sisters were different. Holly was sweet and a little scattered. I was the responsible, steady one - the boring one, Rose liked to say. Rose was the authoritative one. She was bossy and headstrong, but I knew Rose well enough to know that buried under all of her control issues was a heart of pure gold. You just had to dig really deep to find it.

I sighed and followed her into the kitchen. The store wouldn't open up for another two hours and Rose never stayed that long. "Where are the twins?"

Rose busied herself with pouring two mugs. She slid one over to me and doctored hers up with the tiniest bits of cream and sugar. "They're with Matt this morning. I have a doctor's appointment and then some errands to run."

The word doctor made me raise my eyebrows. "Everything okay?"

Rose rolled her eyes. "Yes. Nothing to worry about. We're trying to get life insurance policies and they need some blood work. I should be in and out within five minutes."

Relief shot through me. We might not always get along, but she was my sister and I loved her.

Rose took a sip of her coffee. "Where's the old bag of bones?"

She'd never called Harry by his given name and preferred to refer to him as many different objects - all involving bones.

"No idea," I muttered. Sometimes Harry was here. Sometimes he chose to hide in the back. He wasn't Rose's biggest fan, but sometimes he came out to visit.

"Was he the one to find the bones in your yard?" Rose asked, her eyes gleaming with interest.

A sigh escaped me. The bones were the most interesting thing to happen in Moonmist in years. I avoided answering her question. "I'm so tired of talking about those bones."

Rose laughed. "You're going to be answering questions about them for months. I saw the police out here yesterday. Did they find anything else?"

I blinked at her. Had they been here? I shrugged. "No idea. They haven't told me anything."

"Weird," Rose pondered. "I wonder who it was. And why they put the bones here. It would seem harder to put them there than just dump them somewhere else. It almost seems deliberate." Her tone was light, but there was a questioning look in her eye.

"I did not murder anyone and try to dissolve the body," I told her, shaking my head. "It's a horrible coincidence."

She held her mug up in a salute. "Remember what Dad always used to say about coincidences?"

There was a pang in my heart at the mention. Dad had passed away a couple of years ago and it hit us hard. We were always so tight knit, but it wasn't until he died that we realized he was the center of the knot. After he passed, we didn't fall apart as much as just ... loosen. I was afraid of what would happen if we didn't start to repair our relationship soon. Rose and I were okay, but we had our moments where we annoyed each other greatly. But Holly and Rose were fractured.

"Oh!" I exclaimed. "I have something for you." I hopped out of my seat and rushed over to the living room where the packages Holly left were. Handing them over, I hesitated before I said something.

The edges of Rose's eyes tightened. "From Holly, I presume," she said lightly, but I could hear the world of hurt in her words. My sister was unforgiving on even the smallest thing. I broke one of her Barbies twenty years ago and sometimes I swore she still held a grudge over it.

"She misses Ava and Archer," I said gently.

Rose's fingers tightened around her mug. "Well, she knows where I live."

We both knew that was a non-answer, but I let it go. I did my best not to get in the middle of this - whatever this was between them. "Okay then," I said diplomatically. I segued into chatting about some of my newer soap recipes. Rose was all ears when I told her about the new calming blend I was coming up with. I packaged up soaps for Ava and Archer and as she walked back down to her car, she waved and smiled. I didn't like my family not getting along, but I'd never met a person who could stay mad like Rose could. I waved and shut the door behind me, only to see Harry standing beside me.

I jumped and clapped my hand over my heart. Normally he sounded like an elephant so I could always hear him. How in the world did I miss his presence this time?

"You were distracted," Harry said helpfully.

Lacey came trotting up to us moments later. I reached down to scratch her behind the ears, and it was then I realized she hadn't bothered to get up and bark when Rose showed up. Lacey wasn't the biggest fan of my oldest sister, but usually she got up to greet her. Not this time, I guess.

Rose got into her car and drove away. I watched her car until it disappeared, feeling oddly sad. I wasn't the kind of person who believed everyone got a happy ending, but I also hoped we would get through this. We'd lost Mom and Dad. I couldn't bear losing my sisters, too.

7

─────

I was hauling in massive containers of coconut oil and bottles of olive oil when the police cruiser pulled up. I set the twenty-pound bucket down and pushed a strand of hair out of my face. The lights were off on the vehicle which was good news. They must be here to ask me more questions.

Sloane stepped out of the vehicle and my heartbeat picked up a little at the sight of him. His face was blank and apprehension trickled down my spine. He was a difficult man to read even on a good day, but this seemed like he was here for business only.

"Miss Bradshaw," he said as he walked up. The passenger door of his cruiser opened and out poured a man I would rather I never saw again. Renny Hawke. He was tall and lean, his jaw sharp as glass, and his wit was even sharper. He'd been the bane of my existence during junior high and high school. I had no idea he was on the police force because I rarely had to deal with them. I shut my eyes for a brief moment and shot a prayer up to anyone who might be listening. When I opened my eyes, Sloane was giving me a considerate look. His gaze slid over to Renny who was heading our way, a slow grin forming on his face when he realized whose home he was at.

"Well I'll be," Renny declared, his slow southern accident sliding like honey against my skin. "If it isn't Miss Ivy Bradshaw." His smile was just as white and wide as I remembered and his eyes were just as crystal blue as they were when we were kids. I used to fantasize about marrying Renny. We'd have three kids - two boys and a girl, and all of them would have those eyes.

When I really got to know him, those fantasies dried up like fruit fallen off the vine. He wasn't a bad person. He was just ... Renny. Too much of everything.

"Hello, Renny," I said politely. I didn't stare at him too long or acknowledge him in any other way. This was not an ideal meeting. The last time I saw Renny he'd been kissing my best friend. Well. Former best friend.

At the tender age of sixteen, it'd felt like my heart had been stomped on and set on fire.

"How've you been, little flower?" he asked. The endearment felt like sandpaper against my skin. He called me that from the time we were in junior high until the day I caught him stepping out. I bristled. Sloane's gaze was heavy on my skin. "I've been wonderful," I said, my voice coming out a little sharper than I intended it too. "What's this about Officer Kramer?" I turned my attention to Sloane, putting my back to Renny. His gaze was on my neck. I could feel it.

Sloane's lips thinned. He didn't like ... whatever this was. I suspected Sloane didn't like being surprised. Neither did I, and I'm sure the surprise was a lot worse for me than it was him. "I'm here to ask you some questions about the deceased." He looked around. "It might be better if we go inside."

"Of course." I eyed the bottles and buckets I still had to unload. To my surprise, Renny stepped forward and took two of the buckets.

"Where do you want these?" he asked.

"Inside." I pointed. "Just inside the door. I can put

them away later."

"Nonsense," Renny said. "You must have a shop in there." A grin touched his face. "I didn't put two and two together to realize you were the one who took this house over. A soap shop. I guess I shouldn't be surprised."

I didn't respond, but I picked up one of the buckets to carry inside so I could make sure Renny wasn't snooping around in my house under the guise of putting the buckets away. Sloane grabbed the olive oil and shut my trunk.

Once we were inside, I led them back to my shop. Renny whistled long and low. "Dang, little flower, you have quite the set up here."

I wish he would stop calling me that. "Thanks," I said shortly. I directed them over to the corner and they both put their loads down. "I appreciate the help. Do you want some tea or anything?" I led them out of the office and into the kitchen. "You can have a seat."

"Do you have any of that blend your mom used to make?" Renny asked, looking far too comfortable at my table. He was talking about the hibiscus and rosehip tea. By itself, it was a little too sour for me. But with a little vanilla and a little sugar, it was a tropical treat. I still drank it all the time.

"I do." I looked over at the other officer who was watching us with an unreadable look on his face. "Officer Kramer?"

He shrugged. "Might as well," he said. "Thanks, Miss Bradshaw."

A pang of disappointment hit me as I realized he'd stopped calling me Ivy. I poured both of them a cup of the already sweetened tea and pushed the glasses over. Sloane's face when he realized the tea was pink almost made me laugh, but I figured he wouldn't appreciate it.

Renny took a long drink and sighed. "I've missed this," he said.

"I'll give you the recipe," I retorted.

He tsked. "But little flower, it tastes so much better when you make it." His gaze was heavy on me. I glared at him and when he grinned at me, I rolled my eyes.

Sloane cleared his throat and shot a heated glance at Renny. "We're here to discuss the bones found in your backyard." He pulled a pen and a small notepad from his pocket.

"Okay." I looked between them. "I'm not sure what there is to discuss, though. I told you everything I know."

Sloane's expression didn't change. "The victim is

named Michael Harper. Does that name mean anything to you?"

I blinked at Sloane as my blood ran cold. "Michael?" I whispered. My heart sped up and I put my hand on my chest as I struggled to breathe. "It can't be," I said, suddenly glad I'd pulled a chair out and sat down.

"You knew him?" Sloane asked.

I nodded, unable to speak for a moment. "He - he comes in here all the time. I - I make a specific soap for gardener's and he buys it all the time. He's not a gardener, but he works with wood all the time so his hands are super dry ..." My voice trailed off. Michael Harper was a kind man. He never had a harsh word for anyone and every time he came in, he brought me something either from his kitchen or a piece of wood he'd whittled. Tears sprang to my eyes. "That's a real shame," I said quietly. "He was one of my best customers and a friend." I made a gentle soap and a balm that Michael always bought. He told me once he'd never had anything ever work as well for him as my products did. I don't know if he realized that magic was being used, but it didn't matter to him. He was loyal to me and my shop, so I was constantly giving him little freebies of new recipes or salves I'd created.

Silence fell in the kitchen. Renny reached over and placed a hand on my arm. "I'm sorry, Ivy." And it sounded like he meant it. That was the thing about Renny. You never knew when he'd disarm you with kindness or when he'd try to make out with your best friend.

I pulled my arm away and nodded. "Is there anything I can do?" I asked. "I can try to help any way I can."

Sloane's expression was careful. "When was the last time you saw him?"

I tried to think back. "I think it was a couple of weeks ago. He came in once a month usually. I tried to get him to buy more soap so he wouldn't have to come so often, but he didn't want to hear of it. He said he liked coming into the shop. It had good energy." I knew I was babbling. I couldn't help it. "What happened to him?" I whispered to Sloane.

"We aren't sure yet," he admitted. "The Forensic witches were more concerned with identifying the victim first so his next of kin could be notified. Now that it's done, they're working on figuring out how he died. Is there anything else you can tell us that might help?"

I thought about the lye missing from my cabinet.

"Well," I began, "my assistant Piper was over here the other day and noticed we were missing some lye."

Sloane stopped writing. His gaze lifted to mine. "How much lye?" His words were short and clipped.

"I'm not sure. Maybe twenty pounds? At least one box."

Even Renny was sitting up straighter. "When did you notice it was missing?" he asked. The laconic tone was gone from his voice. Renny was all business now.

"Like I said, I didn't notice. Piper did. That was ..." I thought about it for a moment. "Two days ago, I think?"

"The same day you found the body?" Sloane asked, his tone a little sharper than it had been a moment ago.

I nodded. "But I had no idea it was a body. I thought it was odd, yes, but there was no way for me to know what it was." Unless I had a six-foot skeleton who watched too much crime television.

Sloane and Renny made eye contact, and I didn't like the look they gave each other. "Umm. What is going on? You can't possibly think I had anything to do with this." I scoffed at the ridiculousness at it all. "I'm a soap maker not a -" I paused. I could see how they felt. I didn't have to guess at what they were feeling. I opened up my senses. Sloane was feeling cautious and something else I couldn't identify. It was like he was discomfited over something. He was also suspicious. Of me. A sigh escaped me. I focused on Renny. He wasn't suspicious of me, but he was worried. "I'm not a criminal," I said. Even though they were making me feel like one.

Sloane tossed the rest of his tea back and stood. "Miss Bradshaw, we'd like to encourage you not to go too far. There are still a lot of things to be uncovered here, but since Michael was one of your best customers and you saw him more than a lot of other people in his life, we can't rule you out."

My mouth dropped open. "You cannot be serious," I blurted. "I have a spotless record in this town. I've never harmed a fly!"

Renny put a cautioning hand on my lower back as he stood. "It's just for a little while," he cautioned. "Just until we find out who's really responsible for his death."

"It was most certainly not me!" I said, my words heated.

"We aren't saying it is," Renny said. I saw Sloane open his mouth to speak, but he shut it just as fast. His jaw was clenched. They thought I was guilty. Of all the harebrained things to happen to me, being accused of murder wouldn't have been in my top ten.

This felt so insane I almost started to laugh out loud. The last thing a soap maker wanted was to lose one of her best customers! I took a deep breath and tried to approach this rationally. When in doubt, appeal to their logic, right? "Michael Harper was one of my best customers. I'm a small-town crafter and the absolute last thing one of us wants is to lose one of their regulars." A sigh escaped me. "I can see how this looks bad. I'm missing a box of lye and someone winds up dead in my backyard." I threw my hands up in the air. "But I hope you can both see I probably wouldn't be that dumb."

Renny snorted with amusement. He knew me well enough to know I wouldn't murder someone and leave them on my property, but he also knew I wouldn't actually murder someone either. Sloane, on the other hand, had no such qualms about putting me at the top of his suspect list.

"Like I said, Miss Bradshaw," Sloane said as he stood up, "make sure you stick around until this is over."

Renny gave me a long look and followed Sloane. I didn't bother showing either one of them out.

8

I woke up the next morning a woman with a mission. I needed to find either the missing lye or who stole the lye. It might be hard to get the information from the place I bought it at due to privacy, but if Callie were working, she might see fit to bend the rules at least a little if I told her what the police suspected about me.

I threw on a pair of skinny jeans and an off the shoulder sweater and padded into the kitchen to grab a quick breakfast. Lacey, with her belly already full with her breakfast, lounged at my feet while I scarfed down some Greek yogurt. The doorbell rang as soon as I'd finished up and Lacey walked with me to the door.

"Sit," I told the pup and she did immediately. I sent a silent thanks to my trainer for doing such a good job. Clasping the leash to her collar, I opened the door.

Charlie stood outside and I handed the leash over. Bending down to scratch Lacey, I plopped a kiss on her fuzzy forehead. "Be a good girl," I told her just before she swiped a huge puppy kiss on my face.

I laughed and swiped the drool from my cheek. "Have fun, you two," I said and waved as Charlie picked the pup up. He held her like a baby, just like she loved.

"We will. I'll see you around eight, Miss Bradshaw."

As soon as they were gone, I yelled out a goodbye to Harry who'd been making himself scarce the last couple of days and headed out to Moonmist Craft Supply.

The building housing the craft supply wasn't much to look at. It sat on the outskirts of Moonmist and was a large aluminum building with a hand painted sign out front. It wasn't until you wandered inside that things became impressive. There were times when I came here just to browse through all their offerings. I rarely escaped without a good dent in my pocketbook.

To my relief, Callie was manning the front desk when I walked in. The doors had just opened so there weren't any customers yet.

"Oh thank goodness," I said as I hurried up to her.

Callie's dark eyes twinkled. "I can honestly say I've never had anyone that happy to see me before."

I laughed and plopped down on the stool beside the raised platform she sat behind. "I have a ..." I paused as I tried to figure out the right word. "Dilemma. I'm not sure you can help me."

Callie's expression became interested. "Does it have anything to do with that body found out on your property?"

Of course Callie would know. Everyone knew by now. "As a matter of fact, it does. Right before it happened, we discovered a missing box of lye from my shop."

Callie's brow furrowed. "Okay. I'm not sure what that has to do with anything."

So, she hadn't heard the rest of it. "They didn't discover an actual body," I told her. "It was bones. Lye was used to try to dissolve the body, but they missed some." Even saying it made me feel sick.

But Callie had no such qualms. "Oooh," she said

with wide-eyed interest. "This sounds like a made for tv movie."

"Well, normally I'd love those, but the police think I had something to do with it."

Callie laughed long and hard until she realized I was serious. Her chuckles slowed and stopped as she regarded me. "No." She shook her head with disbelief. "Impossible. Everyone knows you here and they know you aren't capable of something like that." A bitter expression appeared on her face. "Maybe they should look at some of these new people who are coming into this town, you know?"

We did have a large influx of new people who'd moved into Moonmist, but I always tried to be an optimist. I didn't want to believe anyone could do something like this, but it was obvious. Someone had and if I didn't try to figure out who it was, I might wind up in the Moonmist jail - sooner rather than later. "I don't know who could be responsible. I like to think it wasn't any of us, you know?" Magic users were of a gentler nature than others - most of us, that is. We're creators, dreamers, healers. We weren't murderers or criminals. This was one of the reasons the local police department was so short-staffed.

Callie's lips twisted to the side as she pondered this. "I didn't grow up here," she admitted after a moment. "I came after I graduated college. Moonmist is a much more peaceful town than where I came from, but I saw people I never would have expected doing things I never thought they'd do. I think a lot of times crimes are due to opportunity. Maybe that's what happened. Maybe the victim angered someone and they just snapped."

I couldn't believe that. I'd never seen Michael Harper anger anyone. "I'd have a hard time believing Michael had any enemies." It wasn't out of the realm of possibilities and maybe I should stop being so short-sighted. I only knew him from the shop and sometimes when I saw him around downtown. We'd never discussed things of a personal nature. Not really. I knew he was married, though I'd never met his wife. He didn't have any children and he made his living selling his woodworking pieces.

"You never know the things people keep hidden," Callie said ominously. "Tell me how I can help you."

"I'd like to know if there's a list of people who are buying lye. Was there a shortage recently that could explain why mine was stolen?" I thought about it. "I lost a twenty-pound box. Piper noticed it when she brought in the mica supply. It just seems to be a really odd thing to steal."

Callie nodded, though her expression was uneasy. "I'm not supposed to be giving out that information," she said, her voice regretful. "We do a brisk business in lye sales, but it isn't limited to Moonmist. We have crafters from other areas coming in all the time to purchase it."

I shook my head. "I'm just interested in Moonmist right now. I suspect the guilty party is from here." I didn't know why, but my senses were telling me the culprit lived here.

"Hmm." Callie tapped her chin then leaned over to look at the window. My car was still the only one in the parking lot. "Hang on." She got up and headed toward the back. When she returned, she held a large black ledger. Callie flipped it open and ran her index finger down the page. "Looks like we've had three people buy lye during the last month." She pulled a sticky note out and wrote their names down before handing it to me. "I'd be hard-pressed to believe any of these people had anything to do with it, but you never know." She shut the book and studied me. "There's one other thing you should know."

Over the last few days I'd found out way more

than I needed to know about lye, murder, and magic. I wasn't sure I wanted to know any more.

"Someone has been sniffing around town asking about you and your soap." Callie frowned. "She came in here the other day asking what kind of lye you bought." She rolled her eyes. "We only carry two kinds and they're both exactly the same. But she wouldn't drop it. She wanted to know what kind of mica colors you were purchasing and the type of oils. If I hadn't stopped her, she probably would have tried to figure out what your recipes were, too."

Anger flared within me. There would always be copycats in any business, but it was even more hurtful when you lived in a small town and someone tried to copy you then. A big business could put up with a lot of mimicry. If it happened to my business, it would take money right out of my pocket. "Do you know who it was?" I asked.

She shook her head. "I've never seen her before. I'd recognize her again if I saw her, though." Callie frowned and shook her head. "Bad business there. She's looking to set up shop, I think, and is looking to take your business down."

"Maybe," I said. "I hope she'd have to work a lot harder than asking a few questions to put me out of business." I'd been open less than a year, but in that time, I'd built up a good portfolio of customers. It wasn't only the soap I was selling. I sold magic in a way. They knew if they bought my product, it would work. Something occurred to me. "You didn't happen to catch her name, did you? Was it Trinity?"

Callie's eyes narrowed as she thought about it. "I don't think she said it." She shrugged. "Sorry. She had blonde hair if that helped."

It did. Trinity had blonde hair. The odds of two people in this town asking around about my business were too low for this to be a coincidence. "No matter," I said. I tucked the sticky note into my purse and stood. "Let me buy you lunch sometime," I said. "We need to catch up."

Callie smiled. "I'd like that. I'll give you a call sometime next week."

"It's a date." I made sure I had my purse and left the store. I needed to get back to my shop in time to get it open, but tomorrow I planned to visit everyone on the list Callie had given me.

THERE WERE two customers standing outside my home when I got back - twenty minutes before it opened. I smiled apologetically at both of them, even though they knew it wasn't time for me to open, and went inside, being sure to lock the door behind me. It wouldn't take me long to open, but I didn't want customers trailing after me before I gave everything a once over.

"Thank the gods you're back!" Harry said, rushing over to me as soon as I opened the door.

Startled, the keys dropped from my hand and hit the floor with a loud bang. "Harry!" I clasped my hand over my chest and tried to still my beating heart. "What in the world!"

He waved a hand at me in annoyance. "Someone was trying to get into the shop!"

I bent down to pick up the keys and frowned at him. "A customer?"

He shook his head. "No. Someone was trying to jimmy the lock. They ran before I could get to the door. I must have startled them when I started moving around in here."

That was odd. "Did you see what kind of car it was or anything?"

He shook his head. "They must have been on foot. I heard someone on the porch, then I heard them messing with the lock. When I made it to the window, they were gone."

"Hmmm," I said. I wondered if I should call the police. "I'll take a look at the doorknob when I open. I didn't see anything wrong with it when I came in."

"You should call Sloane!" Harry said. "He'd know what to do."

I'd rather stab myself in the eye. "There's no need to call him, not now that they're gone. I'll check it out and see what needs to be done once the shop slows down."

Harry sighed, a deep and aggrieved sound before he lumbered away. "Some owner you are. They could have robbed you blind!"

I snorted and shook my head. I felt ill at ease, but robberies rarely happened here in Moonmist. Maybe it was someone who was just trying the door handle to see if we were open and Harry got spooked. I tried to put it out of my mind as I walked around checking the register to make sure I had enough change and that all my stock was good to go.

Piper was due into work in a few hours so I'd have some time to check the store out to make sure we weren't missing anything else.

Less than ten minutes later, I opened the store and let the first few customers in. Over the next few hours, I did a pretty brisk business in soap sales, but I noticed a trend. Three out of five people who came in asked me about bath bombs. I made bath salts and oil mixtures, but I'd never added bath bombs to my store.

With all the people asking me, I thought I'd better sit down and sketch out some recipes. I could also add in bubble bath scoops. It would be a way to bring in some nice, bright colors and try out some new scents. A lot of my offerings were colored with natural herbs and some micas. This would be a good chance to bring in some bright neon offerings and see how the customers react to them.

Piper came in a couple of hours later. I started to smile at her, but it slid off my face when I noticed her. Dark circles were prominent under her eyes and her mouth was pinched. Her blonde hair was in a ponytail, but it seemed thin and listless. There was only one customer in the store, so as soon as she came around the counter, I whispered under my breath.

"Are you okay?"

Piper tucked her purse into the cubby under the register. She gave me a bright smile. A false smile. "I'm good," she said, her voice cheery. "I was out late last night."

I could believe that. Piper was young and Moon-mist had a bustling nightlife, but this seemed like more. I'd never told Piper about my magic. In fact, I'd never told anyone. My customers kept coming back because my products worked and while a lot of them probably assumed there was magic involved, others assumed it had to do with the fragrance blends or herbs associated with them. I never answered either way. Today I'd never been more glad of it because my trusted assistant seemed to be lying to me. Her emotions were a maelstrom and so mixed up I couldn't get a read on any of them.

"Oh," I said and smiled back at her. "Okay. Well, we've already had a pretty busy day..." I proceeded to rattle on about how good the sales were and what we needed to restock soon. "If you think you have it under control, I'm going to head to the back and get started on some new recipes."

Her head jerked up at that. "New recipes?"

"Mmm-hmmm," I said as I began to walk to the back.

"I can help later if you want me to," she offered. "When things slow down."

"That's okay," I told her. "This is merely an experimentation phase for me."

Her eyes flashed disappointment and something else I couldn't put my finger on, but she nodded and turned away.

I watched her for a moment before I headed

back to the workshop. Why was she acting so weird today? And why couldn't I pin down her emotions? There were way too many for me to sort through. I shook my head as I started opening cabinets to pull out supplies. I'd try to catch Piper when her shift ended to see if she needed anything.

9

I was giddy like a schoolgirl in the throes of a first crush. The bubble scoops I'd made looked just like scoops of ice cream and smelled delightful. I'd made a butter pecan scent and a cranberry delight. Next to those I'd made two different kinds of bath bombs: Warm Vanilla and Tropical Bliss. My workshop smelled like a beach vacation right now and I stood there with my hands on my hips grinning at my work like a loon. The customers were going to love them.

Piper came in just as I was taking my apron off. Her gaze went straight to the work on the counter and her eyes gleamed. She walked over and leaned over to smell them. "These are amazing," she gushed.

"Did you come up with this by yourself or did you follow a recipe?"

I snorted. "I always formulate my own recipes, Piper. You know that."

A smile played on the edge of her lips and I was glad to see she looked a little better than she had when she'd first come in today. "I do," she acknowledged. "Do you want me to put those recipes away?"

I shook my head. I hadn't written them down yet because I was still experimenting. "No need. I'm happy with these but they're a work in progress."

"How long until they can be used?" she asked.

"I'd give it three full days and then we can test." Testing was the best part of my job. It meant a wonderful soak in the clawfoot tub I'd spent an arm and a leg to install.

"Can't wait," she said and though her voice sounded excited, her emotions flared with worry.

"Piper," I said slowly, "are you sure everything is okay?"

"Hmm?" she stood. "Oh." She blinked. "Yes. Of course. Sorry. I'm just having an off day."

"If you need to talk to me about anything, I'm here," I told her. "If you need any time off or anything, I'd be happy to grant it."

Piper's eyes flared wide. "No," she said in a hurry. "I don't need any time off." She paused and I could see her collect her thoughts. "But I appreciate it, Ivy. I really do." Her shoulders sank and she bowed her head.

Something worse than a late-night was up with my assistant. I gave her a long look. "Okay then. Just let me know."

Piper nodded and hurried out of the room.

So weird, I thought. She was always so upbeat and happy so to see her like this was odd. Hopefully she'd trust me enough to tell me soon. I couldn't have her coming into work like that every day.

Shaking my head, I flipped off the lights of the workroom and kicked off my shoes on the way to the bedroom. It was time for lounge clothes and a nice dinner.

THE NEXT MORNING, I was out the door by nine a.m. I'd left Harry brooding in front of the television with Lacey curled on his lap. My pup was scared of a lot of things but not a walking, talking skeleton. How that made sense, I had no idea. I had the note Callie scrawled for me and the addresses of two of the businesses. The other one didn't appear to have a business yet, but her address was easy enough to find in the Moonmist directory. I wasn't sure how I'd approach her yet. Showing up at her house demanding to know about a lye purchase seemed intrusive at best.

The first person was Mark Rourke. I'd never met him, but I knew a few people who'd used his business when they were having plumbing problems. I pulled up to the Up a Creek plumbing company, cracking a smile when I saw the sign out front. It depicted a man in a rowboat and water flaring up all around him. A chime sounded when I walked into the building and an older woman who sat at the front desk greeted me.

"May I help you?" she asked.

I plastered on a polite smile. "Yes, I'd like to see Mark Rourke if he's in please."

"In what regards?" The woman seemed pleasant enough but she hadn't cracked a smile yet.

"I'd like to ask him about lye," I said. It was honest and yet didn't tell the whole truth.

The woman's eyebrows rose but her face had no expression. "I'm sure I can help you," she said. "I'm familiar with all the chemicals we use."

I'm sure she was but I needed to be able to read Mark's emotions. "I'd like to speak with Mr. Rourke directly if at all possible."

The woman's lips thinned. "He's indisposed."

"I can wait," I said, knowing it would make her angry.

"He won't be back in until late this afternoon." Her eyes gleamed with victory.

"Margaret!" A man called from the back. "Is that my package?"

Her eyes went wide and a pale flush of color coated her cheeks.

"Mr. Rourke, I presume?" I asked and brushed past her to the back.

The sound of her chair squeaking followed me.

"Mr. Rourke?" I called. I sped up my steps so she couldn't catch me before I found him.

I rounded a corner only to bump into the man himself. "Oh!"

He caught me by the arms. "Steady there," he said. "No plumbing emergency is worth an accident," he said, his voice light and jovial.

"Mark!" the woman exclaimed. "She pushed her way back here!"

Mark's eyes narrowed a little as he studied me. He let go of my arms once I'd righted myself. "I'm assuming this is a plumbing emergency?"

I nodded at first, then shook my head. "Yes. Well, no. But it is kind of an emergency."

Mark walked over to a small round table with a few chairs scattered around it. "Please," he said, gesturing to one of the chairs.

We both sat down and I took a deep breath. This was awkward and a little weird and he might not talk to me once I told him why I was here, but I was going to say it anyway. "Mr. Rourke, my name is Ivy Bradshaw. I run a soap shop deeper in town and I'm here because of some lye you purchased."

"Mark," the man said automatically. "You can call me Mark."

I leaned forward. "There was a body found on my property." I shut my eyes for a second in frustration. "Bones, I should say. The body was dissolved using lye."

Mark's eyes went wide and he blinked a couple of times. "Lady, I have no idea what that has to do with me."

"The police think I might be responsible for it. I'm trying to track down who has purchased lye over the last couple of months."

Mark shook his head. "We purchase lye all the time because we use it to clean drains." A chuckle escaped him. "You sound like a crazy person, you know that?"

I had to laugh. I must sound insane. "I'm sorry," I

said, and I meant it. "It's just it seems like they're trying to pin something on me that I had nothing to do with."

His expression went thoughtful and I realized Mark Rourke had very kind eyes. He wasn't handsome in a traditional way, but he had an expressive, friendly face with a strong jawline and dark eyes. His face was tanned from outside work and possibly some family heritage, and he had strong, calloused hands. "You know, I think I heard about that," he said after a moment.

"If you hadn't, you'd be the only one in Moonmist," I muttered.

"That's a terrible way to go," Mark said. "I wish I could help, but the only thing we use lye for is in our day-to-day business. I've got records going back the last ten years showing how frequently we have to buy it."

I sighed. "You haven't had any come up missing lately, have you?"

Mark's brow furrowed. "Can't say that I have." He looked over his shoulder. "Margaret!"

The older woman came back around the corner, her lips pinched in disapproval. "Yes?" Her words were short and clipped.

"We haven't had any theft lately?"

Margaret blinked. "No," she said slowly.

"Nothing with any of the lye?"

"Not at all," Margaret said, her voice firm. The woman's disapproving gaze lingered on me. "Is there anything else?"

Mark shook his head and she disappeared again.

"I don't think she likes me," I said.

Mark laughed, a nice low sound. "I can't say she likes anyone who bursts through her self-imposed security and tries to find me."

"I really needed to talk to you," I admitted, color flaring in my cheeks. "I'm sorry I burst in here looking like a crazy woman.

"No need to apologize. But I'm afraid I can't help you. We purchase lye all the time and I solemnly swear I've never used it to remove evidence of a crime."

I snorted with amusement. "Well, then I guess I can cross you off my list then."

"Good," Mark said and stood. He offered a hand to help me up and, surprised by the gesture, I took it. His hand lingered on mine for a moment before letting go. "It was nice to meet you, Miss Bradshaw." Mark reached into his pocket and withdrew a business card. "Don't be a stranger. Call me anytime you want to accuse me of a crime."

A surprised laugh bubbled from me as I tucked the card into my purse. "I will but hopefully there won't be a next time."

We said our goodbyes and I left the building. Margaret didn't bother to say anything to me as I walked out the door, so I didn't bother saying good-bye. A smile tilted my lips and didn't leave until I'd pulled into the next stop - a restaurant called Magic Molly's. The woman who owned this store was named Betty Hope. I'd never been to her restaurant before, but I hoped she would be able to help. This was beginning to feel pretty hopeless, but I couldn't sit idly by while the police worked to build a case against me.

I walked in and was pleasantly surprised by the atmosphere. The smell of apple cinnamon greeted me and I inhaled, pleased to note the scent was not the terrible fake cinnamon sometimes used in bath and body products. This appeared to be the real deal and my stomach grumbled for a slice of apple pie. A young woman, pretty and dark-haired, greeted me. "Welcome to Magic Molly's. Would you like a table or are you just browsing right now?"

She referred to the store connected to the restaurant area, and I realized I did want to browse. I decided to talk to Betty first then check out the store's offerings. "I'm looking for Betty Hope. Is she here today?"

The woman blinked in surprise. "Oh, you're in luck. She usually stops by once a week to check how things are going, so you'll be able to catch her before she leaves. If you wait here a moment, I'll get her."

I nodded and while she was gone, I took the opportunity to check out some of the store's offerings. They sold apple and pecan pie and other delicious looking dessert items, but they also sold candles and clothing. My eye caught something familiar and I was just about to walk over when the hostess returned with an older woman dressed in a flannel shirt and a pair of jeans.

She had a polite but quizzical expression on her face. "Hello," she said and extended her hand. "Betty Hope."

"Ivy Bradshaw," I said. The woman's expression didn't change, so it was obvious she had no idea who I was. "I'm here to ask you a few questions about some lye."

Betty's brows knit together, but she shook her head as she walked into the restaurant. "We can grab a table. I'm not sure how much I'll be able to help you, but I can try."

I sat down and ordered a cup of coffee and a slice of apple pie.

Betty beamed at my order. "It's the best pie in three states. I hope you enjoy it."

I patted my stomach. "I'm sure I will. I've yet to meet an apple pie I didn't like."

Betty ordered her own cup of coffee and when the waitress left, she put her hands on top of the table and crossed them. "Now tell me what this is all about."

I quickly explained the situation and when I told her where I was, I realized she'd already heard about the body.

She nodded and when I'd finished, she spread her hands out. "We do use lye, honey, but it's for our pretzels."

I blanched. "Your ... what?"

Betty laughed then, a warm sound. "We make German pretzels and pretzel bites. A quick dunk in lye gives them that nice hard and shiny crust."

I sat back and stared at her. "Are you serious?" I'd never heard of anything like that in my life.

Betty's friendly face creased in a wide smell. "Totally. I might have culinary magic, but sometimes it's the mundane things that make all the magic. Baking soda, baking powder, sugar, flour. Those are just small things by themselves. But put together? That's when the mundane magic happens. Lye is used in a lot of things, but a lot of people don't know it's used in food as well. I wish I could help you, honey, but we only purchase small amounts of it. The pretzels are good sellers all year, but it only takes a little when we use it for the pretzels."

By then our coffee and my pie had arrived. I tucked into it and shut my eyes in bliss. "You're right," I said. "This is the best pie I've had in three states."

"It's our secret family recipe," she stated proudly. "Our apple pie is one of a kind."

Betty waited for me to finish up and waved her hand at me when I tried to pull money out to pay. "My treat," she said. "I haven't had the chance to sit down and just chat in a while." She winked at me. "Plus, the look on your face when you realized what I used my lye for made the cost of it worth it." Betty stood and chuckled.

I followed her, but on my way out, I detoured to check out the bath and body section. I was just coming up on the lotions when something made my heart lurch. I swayed on my feet. Betty came up beside me and when she saw what I was looking at, she smiled.

"Oh, these are just my favorite, you know?" She picked one up and held it to her nose. Betty inhaled and shut her eyes. "Just smelling these ... they just make my shoulders drop, you know? And our customers love them."

My soap. She'd just picked up a bar of my soap. How in the world had it gotten in here and why didn't I know about it?

"Umm. Betty? Where did you get this soap from?"

"You're interested, too?" She laughed. "I bet. Everyone loves it." She thought for a moment. "The store manager here was the one who set the deal up. I think we order every few months. I'll have to ask her. I saw the woman once, but I'm not sure I'd know her again if I saw her." At last, she saw my thunderous expression. "Umm. Ivy? Everything okay?"

"Everything is fine," I said through clenched teeth, "but this is the same soap I sell in my shop and I know I didn't sell it to you."

Betty's eyes widened. "Oh. Oh my." Her expression fell. "Well, I guess we ought to take this off the shelves then, shouldn't we?" She began to reach for it and I stopped her.

"No. Just keep everything the way it is." An idea formed in my head. "But when you're ready to accept the next shipment can you let me know?"

Betty's eyes crinkled at the edges. "Oh, that's smart," she breathed. "I think she's supposed to be here in a couple of days, but I'll verify that. I'll check with the store manager to see if we can get the seller's details, too."

"I really appreciate it," I told her. I took one of the bars and was about to head up to the register to pay for it. Betty put a hand on my arm. "No. Go ahead and take it."

I gave her a grateful smile. "Thanks. This is definitely my recipe and my bar, but I wanted to take one back home with me." I wanted to see if maybe my next-door neighbor could reverse engineer it to track it back to the person who took it.

"Good luck, Ivy. I hope to see you again." She winked at me. "We have that apple pie every day."

I groaned. "You'll have to roll me out of here if I come back too many times," I joked as I lifted my hand in farewell.

I was supposed to go to two more places today, but the soap discovery upset me so much I headed back home. The store was closed today, so I didn't have to deal with any customers. Thank goodness for that. I wasn't sure I could deal with anyone without wanting to scream. Who in the world was selling my soap right out from underneath me and even more than that, how had they gotten their hands on it?

Trinity Blackwood. It had to be Trinity. How'd she gotten into my house, I had no idea. That woman had been single-handedly copying everything I did since we were younger. I wouldn't put something so egregious past her. I let out a deep breath and tried to calm myself before my thoughts plunged over the deep end. This wasn't the most important thing right now.

Michael Harper was the most important thing. If I couldn't find out who'd harmed him, there might not be a soap shop anymore because I'd be in the clink.

My fingers tapped on the steering wheel as I drove home, but instead of pulling into my driveway, I pulled into Luna's. I didn't know if my next-door neighbor could help me, but she would probably know who would. I knocked on the witch's door and waited for an answer.

Luna herself opened the door and blinked in surprise. "Ivy!" She held open the door. "I was just making a pot of tea. Do you want some?"

After the day I had? "I'd love some," I muttered.

Luna led me inside. Her house was whimsical, filled with bright pops of color, gemstones, and plants everywhere. I loved coming here. It was like walking into a madhouse filled with joy. She motioned for me to sit down at the table and she poured me a cup of tea that smelled like mint and lavender. Luna plunked down a container of honey and a small ceramic vessel filled with cream. "You look like you've had a bad day," she said, her voice soft and pleasant.

Luna was a slightly plump young woman with dark brown hair and light hazel eyes. There was a dusting of freckles across the top of her nose and her smile was always wide and infectious. Everyone I knew liked her, and I knew her plants loved her. She wore a flower crown of white baby's breath and a maxi dress that dragged on the floor when she walked.

I rummaged through my purse and pulled out my soap. As I pushed it across the table to her, a quizzical expression appeared on her face. "Are you trying to sell me soap?" she deadpanned. "Because I almost spent my entire paycheck in your shop last week."

I snorted. "No. I found this in Magic Molly's. Someone has a deal to sell my soap in there and it isn't me!" Anger filled me again, and I squashed it down.

Luna's lips turned down. "Are you a hundred percent sure it's your soap?" She opened the bundle and shook her head. "Don't answer that. This is your peace soap, isn't it?" She held it up to her nose. "I'd recognize the scent anywhere."

"I don't understand how this happened," I said, frustration making my voice wobble. "My stock isn't low. I haven't noticed any theft. And yesterday I started hearing rumors about a woman asking about my soap business, and it's Trinity Blackwood!"

Luna's hand stilled then. She knew all about my history with Trinity. "You think she's responsible?"

I scrubbed a hand over my face. "She has to be. There's no other explanation. She's been asking about my recipes and trying to get the formulations for them. She wanted to know what type of lye and micas I used." I shook my head. "I still don't know how she managed to get into my shop, though."

Luna's lips twisted to the side as she regarded me. "Perhaps there's more than one person working with her." She took the soap and studied it before she stood. "I'll be right back." Luna rushed over to her apothecary cabinet and took a few things out.

When she returned, she set the items neatly in a row.

"Are you ready?" Luna asked.

I nodded. "Of course I am. All I want to know is the truth."

"Sometimes the truth is the hardest to accept," murmured Luna, but before I could respond, her eyes glazed over and magic began to seep from her fingers. I watched as it trickled into my soap, highlighting the curves and edges of it. Luna's face was slack with concentration and as I watched, the soap slowly began to peel itself until it was in shreds on the table. So much for that bar. Not that I would use it anyway.

Luna inhaled sharply and her gaze came back into focus. She frowned down at the soap and back up at me. "This is your soap," she said after a moment, "but it wasn't made by you."

I stilled, the ramifications of her statement slamming into me with the force of a train. "Wha -" I swallowed hard and tried again. "What does that even mean?"

"It appears someone has your recipes. I can't sense any magic seeping from the soap, so it's simply a bar of soap." Her lips pressed into a tight smile. "If there's any bright spot here, it's that."

I sat back in my chair, stunned. "There are only a couple of people who have access to my soap recipes, but I can't believe either one of them would be responsible for taking them." But as I thought about it, I realized I kept my recipes in my shop, usually right on top of my workspace.

In a box labeled *Recipes*.

A groan escaped me. "Anyone could have taken them," I said. "The box is labeled and they're in my unlocked workshop just a few doors down from the shop."

"Were you able to sense anything else?" I asked.

Luna nodded. "There was a glimpse of blonde hair. Whoever this was is female. She has a slim build."

"Trinity," I said again. Maybe it was time to pay her a visit. "Thank you, Luna. If you want to come to the shop next week, you can have your pick of soap. Whatever you want."

Luna's eyes brightened. "Really? Oooh. This was so worth it then. You might regret you offered," she said laughing.

"Never," I told her with a smile. "I mean it. If you want to come in early before customers get there, just let me know. I can open the shop twenty minutes early for you."

"Best visit ever," Luna said. "I'm sorry I couldn't narrow it all the way down for you."

"You did more than enough," I assured her as I headed toward the door. "I have something a little more pressing to take care of right now, but I'll get to the bottom of this very soon."

I had to. My business depended on it.

10

———

I felt no closer to discovering who'd killed Michael Harper than I had the day Harry found him. My mind spun with all the possibilities as I laid out all of my materials to make new batches of soap. Why would someone hurt a kind woodworker? What could he have possibly done to make someone so angry they would take his life? And why did the killer put him on my property? The only thing I could think of was someone wanting to point the finger at me. It had worked. Somewhat. I wasn't under arrest, but the police were definitely looking into me. But like I told them before - I would never want to harm someone who brought me as much business as he had.

The doorbell rang shortly before 8 a.m. Annoyance fluttered through me at first. Eight was too early for unannounced visitors, but when I rounded the corner, my heart thumped an extra beat.

Sloane Kramer stood outside, this time without Renny. I let him in and noticed Sloane skimming my attire, an amused little smile resting on the corner of his mouth. I didn't dress up to make soap. I dressed down.

I wore a pair of old and faded skinny jeans, beat-up tennis shoes, and a long-sleeved slouchy top. A pair of goggles was perched on the top of my head and over my clothing, I had a durable, black rubber apron. His eyebrows rose. "Am I interrupting something?"

Harry chose that exact moment to interrupt. "Ivy! I swear to all that's holy if you don't stop eating my cookies ..." He paused as he regarded Sloane. "Oh hello. I assume you're here to arrest Ivy for her sweet tooth? It's really putting a damper on my future enjoyment of snacks." He sniffed. "Especially when I go into the cabinet and realize there are no snacks." His jaw clicked shut to emphasize that announcement.

Sloane's mouth dropped open. "Ivy?" he questioned. There was a sharp interest in his eyes. I realized all of a sudden I'd forgotten to ask him about help with Harry. Sam was helping, but he was no necromancer.

"This is Harry. He's ... I'm not quite sure what he is. I've been meaning to ask for your help with him."

Harry sighed like the weight of the world was on his shoulders. "Of course you forgot to ask. Why am I not surprised? It's not like I have anything going on. It's not like I need to know my origins. It's not like -"

"Harry," I snapped. "Stop."

He snorted with derision but stopped his chattering.

Sloane's brows drew together with confusion. "I've never seen anything quite like him," he admitted. "If I had to guess, I'd say he's a trapped spirit." He frowned as he looked him over. "The skeleton appears to just be the vessel he's attached to. It doesn't belong to him so a DNA test wouldn't help." His gaze lifted to Harry's face. "Do you remember why you were trapped?"

The skeleton clammed up and refused to say a word. So, Harry had remembered after all. I wondered what he'd done to be ashamed to even talk about it.

Coming to the same conclusion I had, Sloane nodded. "Anything you could remember would help me. I can't promise much, but I can tap my network and our collective knowledge to see if anyone could help."

Harry nodded. "I'll consider it," he said before he clomped away.

Sloane's gaze followed him out. "Why is it when I come to your house, I always see strange and wonderful things?"

I let my shoulder rise and fall in a shrug. "It's a gift, I suppose." I led him back to my shop. "I have quite a bit to do today. Can I work while we talk?"

Sloane considered me for a moment. "Can you do both?" he asked finally.

"Of course I can. I've been soaping for years." I handed him an extra pair of goggles, an apron, and a pair of gloves. "You can help if you want to."

Sloane considered the items then shrugged. I hid my smile. So the officer wasn't as rigid as I thought he was. As soon as he was geared up, I walked Sloane Kramer through my process.

He watched with avid fascination and when I handed over the stick blender to him for blending, he was like a kid in a candy store.

I'd never had so much fun teaching soap making and we were so into the process, I almost forgot he hadn't asked me any questions. I also realized I hadn't used any of my magic for this batch of soap. I chewed on my lips as I thought about it and whether I wanted to let my secrets slip with him. But Sloane was a necromancer - a person whose magic was sometimes outright shunned. I took the stick blender from him and made sure the soap had achieved trace before I held on to both sides of the bowl. I shut my eyes and concentrated on imbuing the still liquid soap with the properties of relaxation and calming.

Sloane inhaled sharply, but I couldn't focus on him right now. If I did, I'd mess up the entire batch. When I was finished, I said the words of binding and stepped away to grab the smaller pitchers. Sloane's eyes were wide.

I offered him a tight smile.

"Your face glows when you do that," he said. "Did you know?"

I blinked in surprise. "No. I guess I never watched myself."

"It's ..." he swallowed hard. "Amazing," he said after a moment.

Time stretched between us and I thought about my first impressions of him and decided I'd been wrong about the officer. Sometimes our experiences shaped the way we were. I couldn't imagine the world being kind to him with the power of life and death in his hands. "Thank you," was all I said. "It helps people. It's all I ever wanted."

Sloane looked away and cleared his throat. I busied myself with measuring out different amounts of soap in the pitchers and coloring it with gold and dark blue micas.

"You've answered some of my questions already," he said and chuckled. "I was here to ask about your processes, but you've shown me some of them."

I looked up just as I stirred the last of the mica in. "About the lye?"

He nodded. "None of us know much about it."

"Mmm," I agreed. "It's just like I showed you. Mix the lye with the water, never the other way, and use the lye to make soap." I shrugged and laughed. "There's no real mystery to it. I make soap several times a week and order it quarterly from the Moonmist Craft Supply. Callie keeps all the records there if you need to verify."

"Thanks. I think you should know we found out how Mr. Harper died."

I stopped stirring. "I'm not sure I want to know," I said honestly.

"If it helps, we don't think you're responsible anymore." Sloane frowned. "At least not directly."

I held one of the pitchers up high and tilted it,

allowing the now gold soap to fall freely into the uncolored soap, stopping it when I'd poured in about a quarter. I tried not to let the annoyance show on my face. "You don't think I killed him, but you still think I was somehow involved?"

"You're too short. He died of blunt force trauma to the head." Sloane scratched his neck and grimaced. "I still don't understand how Forensic witches can pick all of that up without a body." He shook his head and spoke again. "A woman could have done it, but the angle of it would have made it difficult for you."

"A taller woman or man?" I picked up the blue soap and did the same thing, alternating with both blue and gold until I'd scraped the pitchers clean.

Sloane nodded. "If you can think of anything at all that could help, please call me."

"Of course I will. I don't have any new information. If I stumble over some, I'd be happy to reach out."

Sloane gave me a weird look at that admission, but I was too annoyed to care.

"I'll show myself out then," he said.

I nodded but didn't stop what I was doing. It was only after he'd shut the door that I realized I'd forgotten to scent this batch.

"Crud," I muttered. There was a big market for unscented products, but I usually didn't go to the effort of swirling a design in those bars. Maybe I could get a little extra for these. They should turn out with a unique pattern.

I planned to spend most of the morning in the shop, but I couldn't stop thinking about Sloane's words. The way Michael died didn't seem to indicate rage. Maybe he stumbled on something he shouldn't have? I carefully covered the soap mold with a wooden lid and left it to cure for 24 hours. I'd cut it tomorrow morning, maybe earlier. The shop was due to open in a little while, so I called Piper to see if she'd come in.

"Of course," she said. "I'm always looking to make extra money."

It's why I liked her. She didn't mind coming in and I didn't mind paying her for it. She sounded happier, more upbeat and relief skittered down my spine. I liked Piper and didn't want to see her so unhappy.

She showed up ten minutes before the store opened and just as I was gathering my keys and a jacket. I let her in, rattled off what was going on in the shop today, and headed out right after I told her I might be gone the rest of the day.

There was one person I hadn't talked to. I had no idea whether she would take the time to chat with me or not, but she was one of my last leads.

I SHOWED up at Michael Harper's house less than twenty minutes later. It was a small white home with its shutters printed a cheery bright blue. The porch was well cared for, something I'd expect from a master woodworker like Michael. I grabbed the bag of soap I'd gathered for his wife and got out of my car.

I wasn't sure what to expect from Mrs. Harper. Michael was a kind man, not exactly handsome, but not unpleasant either. It was his kindness that had always drawn me to him. The woman who answered the door was stunning. She was tall with dark hair and bright blue eyes. Her face was drawn with grief and dark circles looked like they'd made a permanent home on her skin.

Her forehead creased when she saw me.

"Hello," I said quickly. "My name is Ivy Bradshaw. I own *The Suds Stop*." I shoved the bag at her. "I'd like you to have this. It might bring you at least some measure of peace during the time."

The woman reached for the bag, her expression

clearing. "You're the soap maker." She held open the door for me. "Please. Come in."

I stepped inside and watched as she opened the bag and inhaled. "These smell wonderful. Thank you so much."

"It was the least I could do." I didn't make the grief blend a lot. Maybe a few times a year. It was a slow seller and for that I was glad. I'd gone through my stock yesterday evening and pulled several bars I thought she might need. One was the grief bar, but I'd also brought her a Restful Night's Sleep bath oil, a fun bath bomb with a bright floral scent, and the Broken Heart soap. I wasn't a miracle worker, but I could help ease someone's pain.

She introduced herself as Helen and offered me some tea. I accepted and waited in her living room until she came back with two steaming mugs. "I admit, you've taken me off guard," she said. "I'm not sure how I can help you, but I'll do my best."

"I'd like to help Michael," I said. "I'm not sure what I can do for him, but I did want to ask if there was anything strange or odd about him before his death?"

Helen sipped her tea, her face contemplative. "The police have already asked this. There was nothing odd about him. He was always kind and rock steady. He wouldn't have hurt a fly, so I can't imagine what this is about."

"Did anything weird happen before his death? Anything at all? Can you think of anything he might have said or done differently than usual."

Helen's lips purse and her forehead wrinkled as she thought, but after a moment it cleared. "No," she said a moment or two later. But then her forehead wrinkled again. "Well. Now that I'm thinking about it. Maybe."

I leaned forward in anticipation. "Anything new you could add would be really helpful."

"He came home a few days before he died and told me he'd found something out about someone. He said it had to do with someone stealing." She shrugged. "I tried to ask about it, but he wouldn't tell me. He also didn't seem overly concerned about it. Just a little bothered. I didn't think too much of it after that."

"Did you tell the police this?" I asked.

She shook her head. "Like I said, I didn't even think about it. I wonder if I should."

I nodded. "I would. Don't leave anything out. Any small thing can help, no matter if you think it's relevant or not."

We drank our tea and chatted for a little while

longer, but Helen couldn't remember anything else strange leading up to the date her husband had died. When I finished my tea, I excused myself and told her if she ever needed any soap, I'd be happy to give her a fifty percent discount for however long she needed it. Tears shimmered in her eyes at my offer. "Thank you so much, Ivy. No wonder Michael liked you so much."

We hugged and once I got into my car, I released a shaky breath. She hadn't been lying. About any of it. Helen was a woman in the throes of genuine grief. It had flooded my senses when she opened the door. But I also sensed great happiness within her when she spoke about her husband. She'd loved him deeply. I suspected Helen would mourn his loss the rest of her life and never marry again. I slowed my breathing and tried to let her emotions wash away from me. It wasn't always easy. Especially when it came to deep grief, but eventually I felt the shadows pass and my breathing became a little steadier with each moment to pass.

I hoped one day I'd love someone that much.

11

───────

Trinity Blackwood still lived in her childhood home. I pulled up next to the curb, my fingers gripping the steering wheel so tight the knuckles went white. Once upon a time, Trinity and I had played hide and seek through the woods in her backyard and ate popsicles on the front porch together. The memory gripped me hard and wouldn't let go. The icy tang of artificial grape in my mouth and the sticky sugar syrup dripping on my knees. Trixie always preferred the cherry ones so her mouth would be bright red for hours afterward.

I wasn't sure I could go up to her door. I wasn't sure I could put my anger and grief over our lost friendship away and try to talk to her reasonably about what was happening.

I knew I needed to. There was only one way to get to the bottom of my soap mystery and it was through her. I turned the car off and slid out of the driver's seat. I felt numb and my limbs moved almost woodenly as I walked up the porch I'd spent so many years on before. Tears sprang to my eyes and I quickly forced them back. The last thing I needed was to show weakness in front of my enemies.

I rang the doorbell, suppressing the urge to run back to my car and speed away.

Footsteps sounded throughout the house and I remembered the wooden floor and how loud it was. There was a board in the kitchen that creaked every time you stepped on it, so Trixie and I would creep around it when we snuck cookies out of the refrigerator.

The door opened and I was face to face with someone I had once loved.

She still looked wonderful. Trim and blond with a pert, delicate nose and a spray of light freckles across her tanned face. Her hair was perfectly styled - blonde and curly. She wore a pair of leggings with a long asymmetrical peach sweater. Her jade green eyes widened in surprise when she was who it was standing on her front porch.

"Ivy?" she questioned, her brows drawn together in confusion. "Is everything all right?"

Her voice was low and husky and the words were spoken with just the right amount of concern. She was always good at fooling people. She'd fooled me until I managed to control my powers. I focused on her emotions today and thought I would find some-thing angry but ... she wasn't. She was confused. And concerned. I didn't want to think about that - didn't want to see she genuinely had no idea why I was here.

I opened my mouth to speak and realized there were a million things I wanted to say. Thoughts of my soap flew right out of my head. What I really wanted to ask her was why. But I couldn't. It was ancient history and neither one of us wanted to talk about it.

"Hi Trinity," I said, surprised to hear the words come out sure and steady. "I'd like to talk to you for a few minutes if that's okay."

"Umm," she said, her green eyes bright in her tanned face. "Sure." She held the door open. "You'll have to excuse the house. Ryder is here today." She toed a stuffed animal out of the way and shut the door behind me. "I'm right in the middle of cutting sugar cookie dough out if you don't mind chatting while I do that."

"Not at all," I said. I had no idea who Ryder was, but as soon as she turned the corner to head into the kitchen, I spotted a towheaded little boy sitting at the kitchen island. Crayons were scattered around him as he concentrated on coloring a vicious looking T-Rex chasing after a poor superhero. My breath caught. I had no idea Trinity had a son. I looked around for evidence of a husband but found none. It didn't mean there was one, but when I caught a glimpse of Trinity's left hand, there was no ring.

I squashed down the empathy threatening to flood me.

"Would you like a glass of water or anything?" she asked.

I shook my head. I really didn't like talking in front of her son, but he was only about two or three so as long as it didn't escalate into yelling, it should be okay. "No thanks. I won't take up too much of your time. You look pretty busy."

Trinity had a massive rectangle of sugar cookie dough laid out on her counter and numerous cookie cutters piled in a bowl. Next to them were several bags of colored icing with different pipes. She shrugged.

"I'm trying to bring in a little extra money this month. My writing work was a little on the thin side this month." She waved at the dough. "It's a lot of work, but I can bring in quite a bit with the cookies I decorate."

"How wonderful," I said politely. I was still trying to squash my empathy for her.

She gave me a tight smile. "I have to admit I'm surprised to see you here."

"I'm surprised to see me here myself," I admitted.

The statement got a laugh out of her. Ryder looked up and gave her a toothy grin before he went right back to coloring. I'd never seen a kid that young be entertained like that especially with a guest around.

"What is it you need?" she asked. "If you don't tell me soon, I'm going to hand you a cookie cutter and put you to work."

Trinity was always funny. The memory made me sad. I sat up a little straighter. "I'm sure you've heard about what happened on my property the other day."

Trinity nodded. "I did. I'm sorry to hear about Mr. Harper. He seemed like a good man." Her emotions seemed true. There was a brief flash of sympathy followed by genuine sadness.

"Me too," I murmured. "He was one of my best customers."

Her eyes flicked up from her work. "I'm not sure what that has to do with me, though."

Here went nothing. "A few people have told me you were asking about my storefront operations and trying to see if you could get my recipes."

Trinity stiffened. Her lips thinned and the skin around her eyes tightened. She stilled for a moment before she began cutting her cookies out again. "I see."

"Well, I've had some lye come up missing and since it was used in Michael Harper's murder..."

Trinity slammed her cookie-cutter down. "Ivy!" Tears filled her eyes. "Do you honestly think I could kill someone?"

I wasn't sure what she was capable of. I never used to think she was capable of it but people changed. She changed more than I ever thought she could. When I stayed silent, she gave one sharp nod of her head and a bitter laugh escaped her. "Of course you do." She gripped the edge of the counter and took a deep breath. Ryder looked up at her, his face beginning to show concern. Trinity stepped around the island and stroked his hair. "Everything is fine, honey." She beamed down at the scribbled T-Rex and praised him for how beautiful it was.

I stood up, unable to bear it anymore.

"Stay, Ivy," Trinity said. She tossed a couple of towels over the dough and started a pot of coffee. "Just for a little while. I'd like to talk to you."

I wanted to decline. I should decline. But Trinity's emotions were all over the place and I couldn't find any falsehood in her statements today. Against my better judgment, I nodded.

Her eyes softened. "Thank you," she said. We waited in awkward silence for the pot to finish but once she made the mugs, she led me outside to a small patio area. Ryder followed behind her with his colors and his book. She set him up at a small table a few feet away. The place wasn't the same as it was when I was a child, but the woods hadn't changed much. I sat at a small round mosaic table. The chair was iron but had padding on the back and bottom of it and was surprisingly comfortable.

I sipped my coffee.

"I had nothing to do with Michael Harper's murder," she said. "Nor did I have anything to do with your missing lye." She watched the woods with a careful eye. "I was asking about you because I'd heard you came home. I wasn't sure where your storefront was."

Truth. She was telling the truth. "I knew your parents had a couple of homes, but I couldn't remember where they were. I didn't want to just show up. When I heard a new soap shop had opened up, I wondered if it was you." She twisted the bottom of her sweater in her hands. "I've been wanting to talk to you for so long and I just - " Trinity shook her head. "I guess I went about it the wrong way. I didn't mean to upset you or make you think I was copying you." A bitter laugh escaped her. "I have my hands full enough now. I can't handle one more to do thing on my list. And learning soap?" She snorted. "With Ryder around? I'd kill us both with the lye."

How was she telling the truth? It had to be Trinity who was stealing my recipes and my lye. If not, who else could it be? I wasn't sure what to say.

"You don't have to say anything, Ivy. I know what you must think of me. For all the things I did to you, if I never said it then, I'd like to say it now. I'm sorry. So very sorry."

A dam broke in my chest then. A wall I'd built around my heart for so many years. I wouldn't cry, though. I wouldn't give Trinity that. She'd stolen my high school boyfriend. But he wasn't just any boy. He was the one I'd always loved. From the time I'd been old enough to know what love was, Cliff was the one for me. If I wasn't doing something with Trinity, I was with Cliff and many times we were all together. But unbeknownst to me, Trinity loved Cliff, too. When I was a junior in high school, I'd found them wrapped in each other's arms in the girl's locker room. It was almost comical how it happened. I never went into the bathroom there. Being sporty or athletic was way out of my wheelhouse. But it just so happened, someone spilled a soda on me on the way to my last class of the day and the locker room bathrooms were the closest. I popped in there in order to clean myself up. I didn't think anything of it when I heard the noise and the whispers. But when I peeked around the corner to where the showers were just to tell them someone had come in, I'd found Trinity and Cliff instead of two strangers, their lips locked together.

My heart shattered that day and even though it was high school, I still hadn't gotten over it. Both of them threw themselves on my mercy, but instead of showing kindness I'd lashed out. I'd noticed over the last year how Trinity would try to dress like me or do the same sports or extracurriculars I did. She started styling her hair like mine and when I finally was able to bring it out and examine it years later, I realized she'd been trying to get Cliff for much longer than high school. I was cruel to both of them just like they'd been cruel to me and I refused to talk to them since that day. I had no idea what happened to Cliff. I never kept up with him. It was too painful. The only reason I knew about Trinity was because people around here talked too much.

"I'm not sure I can forgive you, Trinity. If absolution is what you're searching for, I don't think I can give it to you."

She shook her head. "I don't want anything from you. I just want you to know how much I grieve the loss of our friendship and I would do anything to repair it." Her hands shook before she clasped them together.

A deep sigh escaped me. "You had nothing to do with the lye?" I asked her again.

She shook her head and studied me with wide green eyes.

I nodded and stood, my coffee having gone cold several minutes ago. "Thank you. You've given me a lot to think about."

Her gaze flashed with disappointment but she nodded. "If I hear anything is it ... is it okay if I call?"

Five years ago I might have flown into a rage if

she asked me that. Today I was too exhausted. I nodded instead. "You're welcome to call if you hear anything new."

She stood and led me back to the front door. "Thank you for coming by."

"Goodbye, Trinity," I said. I turned and walked away, not trusting myself to look back.

As soon as I slid into my car, I scrubbed my hands over my face and groaned. Tears sprang to my eyes and I quickly dashed them away.

I was officially back to square one. If Trinity wasn't responsible for the missing lye, then who was? And how was Michael Harper involved in it? With one last look at Trinity's house and a pang of longing for our lost friendship, I started the car and drove away.

12

I drove aimlessly through town for what seemed like hours before I decided to stop by Tiffany Cook's house. Hers was the last name on my list. I vaguely knew of her though I couldn't remember how. Her house was a little less well kept than the others I'd stopped at. Her landscaping was a tad overgrown and the flowers growing in her bed were a little scraggly. I rang the doorbell and waited.

A woman with watery blue eyes and exhaustion lines on the edges of her mouth answered the door. I couldn't place her age. She was anywhere from twenty-five to forty. Her clothing was young - a pair of skinny jeans and jeweled sandals and a flowery top. On her necklace winked what seemed to be a small but real diamond. Her makeup was expertly done, but there was something hard about her.

"Yes?" she barked.

I thought quickly. "Yes, hi, I'm from Moonmist Craft Supply. Once a year we do a door-to-door campaign and try to visit all the customers who've purchased from us before." I pretended to scroll something on my phone. "I was wondering how your lye purchase turned out?" It was lame. I was lame. She was never going to buy this story. The only thing that would save me was how weird Moonmist could occasionally be.

The woman frowned and I thought I was sunk, but just before I could turn tail and run, she jerked a thumb over her shoulder. "I ended up needing more than twenty pounds, so I had to borrow some from a friend of mine." Her words hitched over the word "friend."

"Oh?" I inquired. "Does your friend buy a lot of lye?" I slapped a friendly smile on my face. "We're always looking for new customers!" I said, my voice annoyingly cheery.

"She doesn't," the woman said, "but I think she works for someone who does."

"Ah," I said, even though the world felt like it was going to open up and swallow me. "I see. Well maybe

I'll go visit this woman and see if we can bring her over to our side!"

The woman rolled her eyes and slammed the door on me.

But not before I saw multiple soap molds filled with what looked to be one of my signature soaps. I almost sank to my knees, but she could still be watching me so I turned and walked back to my car trying to seem like I didn't have a care in the world.

Could Piper be involved in this? My brain shuffled through everything I'd learned over the last few days. Piper was taller than me and blonde. Could Callie have mistaken Trinity for Piper? I thought about it. I usually ordered my lye to be shipped to me so it's possible they'd never met. I'd stopped paying attention to Piper's moods unless I really needed to. Like the other day when she was acting so weird.

Maybe stealing from me was the reason for her behavior. If I stole from someone who employed me, I'd certainly be acting shady.

Tears pricked the back of my eyes as I thought about it. Could it be her? And if it was her, how did it relate to Tiffany and with Michael Harper? His widow's words filtered back to me. Michael suspected someone of stealing.

Could Piper be the one stealing my recipes?

My heart ached. I couldn't go back to my shop right now. She was still there. I wondered if she was rifling through my things.

Calm down, I told myself. It's still possible this is all a horrible misunderstanding. Even if she was involved, it didn't explain Michael Harper's death. Stealing from someone and being involved in a murder were two very different things. I hired Piper because she seemed like a good person and I'd paid attention to her for the first few months she worked for me. I saw nothing to be concerned about. But I stopped paying attention once I trusted her and maybe that's when this all started.

My breath was coming in almost panicked gasps right now. I needed to talk to Harry. He might not have put two and two together yet. I needed to talk to Sloane, too.

I turned my car around and headed for the Moonmist Police Department.

To say Sloane was surprised to see me would be an understatement. I burst into the police station and the woman at the registration desk regarded me with cool blue eyes and an unsmiling expression. Before she could greet me, I burst out with, "I'm looking for Officer Sloane Kramer. I'm Ivy Bradshaw and I have information for him. He'll want to see me."

The woman blinked slowly. "Wait one moment, please." She must be used to crazy people coming in blurting out they have information for someone. I gripped my purse tightly against my waist and sat down in one of the uncomfortable plastic chairs they had in the waiting room. Less than five minutes later, Sloane came up from the back, his gaze searching for me. When he saw me, a perplexed look came over his face and he sat down beside me.

"Are you okay?" His voice was gruff but there was genuine concern in his eyes.

I started to speak and felt my lip tremble. A puff of air burst from him and he stood, gently helping me up. "Come with me," he said. Sloane led me to the back and down a hallway filled with cubicles. Some curious glances greeted me, but no one said anything. He opened the door to a small office and ushered me inside.

"Have a seat," he said and plucked a tissue from the box on his desk. He handed it to me and settled himself in his seat.

"Do you have crying women in your office a lot?" I asked as I dabbed my eyes with the tissue.

"You'd be surprised," he said. Sloane steepled his fingers and rested his elbows on the desk. "Tell me why you're here, Ivy."

I inhaled and tried to speak, but my lips went wobbly again. I bowed my head and held up a hand. "Sorry. Just give me a moment."

I heard a shuffling motion and the next thing I knew, Sloane had pulled up a chair and was sitting beside me. "Take your time."

I wiped my leaking eyes with the tissue. "You're a good officer," I said and sniffed.

His chest rumbled with an amused chuckle. "Thanks. I think."

He was. Sloane was a contradiction to me, but he'd shown genuine kindness during our interactions. I took a deep breath and spilled into my story.

"It has to be Piper, doesn't it?" I asked, my heart feeling like it was going to shatter into a million pieces.

He lifted one shoulder in a shrug. "It sounds like it might be, but you can't jump to any conclusions. This might not be linked to Michael Harper at all. It could be two completely separate things."

"But what about the lye? Doesn't it seem like they were the ones who took it?"

"Maybe," he admitted, "but there's almost no way

to trace that either. If Piper was the one stealing your soap recipes, she could also be the one who took your lye. Not for any nefarious reasons, but to use."

There had to be a connection here. I just wasn't seeing how Michael had become involved. He'd suspected someone of stealing something. But how would he have caught Piper taking something? She was always coming in with things for my store and taking out boxes of deliveries.

I put a hand over my eyes and groaned. "None of this makes sense," I muttered.

"Obviously someone is stealing from you," Sloane said. "But we can't go blasting in with accusations on only circumstantial evidence. It doesn't quite work that way." His voice was gentle but firm.

"So I should just go home and pretend nothing happened?" I asked, my voice meek. I wasn't a good actor. I had no idea how I'd pull that off.

"Can you pretend to be sick? Close your shop up for a few days?" Sloane studied me, his gaze still full of concern.

"I don't think so. It would make her suspicious. She's fully equipped to run the store without me. Piper won't understand why she's not allowed to open and close for me."

"Hmmm." Sloane and I fell into silence. He sat up straight. "I have an idea."

"I'm all ears," I said glumly.

"How do you feel about cameras?" Sloane's eyes were bright. "You should probably have them anyway since you live in your store. I could come by..." he checked his watch, "tonight and quickly rig some up. They won't be noticeable. We can see what's going on during the day, especially when you aren't there. If she's hiding something, she won't be able to hide from the cameras."

I thought about it. I didn't want to invade someone's privacy like that, but this was my home, and right now I had every reason not to trust Piper. The odds were she was stealing from me. She was the one who had the most access to my store and my home. After a moment, I nodded. "Okay. The store closes at six and she usually doesn't stay too long."

Sloane reached over and squeezed my hand in a comforting gesture. "I'll be over no later than 7:30. If you can help, that would be great."

"I have no idea how to set up cameras, but I'll do what I can."

"Good," he said. "I can walk you through it. Don't worry, Ivy. We'll do our best to catch whoever this is. Even if it's Piper."

I nodded and left his office a few moments later. I still wasn't ready to go home, so I stopped by Holly's nursery. The Broom and Bloom was a beautiful place filled with a riot of colorful blooms and plants scattered haphazardly around the entire store. I loved it here. Holly's energy was everywhere, but the place itself felt full of life. She'd managed to grow a massive purple clematis and trained it to grow over the arbor customers walked through to get to the front door. I smiled as I walked in, comforted by the sweet scent of blooms and the buzzing of dozens of happy honeybees.

"Holly?" I called as I walked back to the office.

I found my sister hunched over a flat of flowers muttering to herself about the shape they were in.

"Oh!" she said, her eyes widening in surprise when she saw me walk in. She had dirt on her nose and her hair was tied up with a purple bandana. "What a pleasant surprise!"

I walked over and took her into a one-armed hug. She smelled slightly of sweat and dirt. "You look busy," I said as I tossed my purse down on the potting table.

"We got this flat in from one of our nursery supply companies and half of these poor things are near their deathbed!" She shook her head as she studied them. "It would have been less of a hassle for me to grow them myself. It certainly would have been healthier."

I looked over the flat of flowers and saw exactly what she was talking about. Some looked okay, but most of them had grown leggy, their stems too long and their flowers too heavy. "Ouch," I whispered.

"Yeah," she said and sighed. "It's going to take me the better part of the day to fix their growth structure."

Holly was a talented natural mage. She could take any plant and make it bloom. She could make the dirt more fertile or force a tree to fruit. I loved coming here because it was like an extension of her. I just felt Holly here. Her magic was warm and comforting like sunshine on my shoulders. Rose, my other sister, had magic like a misty rain on an autumn day. Two different sides of the same coin. Holly looked up at me.

"You seem troubled," she said as her gaze flicked to the weakened flowers.

"I am," I said. "A lot of strange things have occurred lately and I'm not sure how to handle them."

She stopped finally and studied me before she

nodded, as if she'd made a great decision. "Would you like a cup of lavender lemonade?"

I grinned. Of course Holly would have something like lavender lemonade. "I'd love a glass," I told her.

"Good. It's delicious." Holly walked over to the sink and washed her hands before she pulled two glasses down from the cabinet above her. From the fridge she pulled a glass of slightly purple liquid out. I watched as she mixed a little honey in the glasses and poured the lemonade out. Holly handed me one and I took a sip, pleasantly surprised at the taste. Lavender was a tricky thing to use, but I wasn't surprised she'd managed to nail it. Too much lavender and your food or drink would taste like soap. Too little and you might not taste it at all. The lemons were just tart enough. She'd added just enough honey and the lavender burst into my mouth with a bright floral taste. It was delicious.

"Mmm," I said in appreciation.

"I agree," she said happily. "I made this from the French Lavender batch I harvested last year." She inhaled and sipped her drink. "I used the rest of it to make several batches of unscented soap."

I blinked at her. "I could have given you some."

"I know you could have, but I wanted to make it

myself. I'd never tried it before, but I was pleasantly surprised with how it came out."

I leaned my head on her shoulder, the stress from the last few days rolling off of me in the presence of Holly's comforting light. "I think Piper might be stealing from me," I said.

My sister stilled. "Oh no," she said softly. "Are you sure?"

I started from the beginning, only stopping when Holly got up and poured us more lemonade. When I finished my story, she tapped her fingers on the potting table. "It certainly sounds like she's at least involved in part of it. But do you really think she was involved in Michael's death?" A sad sigh escaped her. "It just doesn't seem like her."

"I know. I'm not sure what to think." I told her about Sloane's camera idea and at first, she looked discomfited about it, but when I told her his reasoning, she sat back in her chair and a contemplative look stole over her face.

"You can try it temporarily and see if it's something you want to keep. If not, you can use it only to see what Piper is doing."

"Yeah," I agreed. I still wasn't a hundred percent comfortable with it, but I'd give it a try. We chatted for a little while longer, and I promised to call her soon.

Back in my car, the trepidation hit me again. I checked the time. It was almost six. I decided to go back to the shop and see if I could handle seeing Piper again.

13

Piper was in high spirits when I walked into the shop. I greeted her with a small wave as I breezed in the door pretending not to have a worry in the world.

"Hey Ivy!" she said. A beaming smile lit her pretty face. She was in a good mood and none of the darkness from the other day lingered around her.

"Hi Piper," I said, careful to keep my voice steady. "How did it go today?" I set my purse down, avoiding eye contact with her. "I'm so sorry I took the entire day. We can work something out with your schedule later if you'd like to make up for it."

"Oh that's okay," she said. "It was pretty busy today. It might have been a good day to introduce those bath truffles," she suggested. "Someone else asked about them today and I couldn't really tell them anything because I didn't know the ingredients."

My mood darkened. "Oh?" I said. "It's easy enough to Google. There are plenty of recipes out there for them."

"But none like yours," she said, but it felt more like probing. "You have some special ingredient no one can figure out."

I poked my head up and looked at her. A wan smile lifted my lips. "What kind of soap maker would I be if I revealed all my secrets?" My voice was light, but my heart was heavy. Just this conversation told me what I needed to know. Piper was the one stealing from me.

"Aww, come on," she pleaded, her voice wheedling. "I've never seen you make your soap from start to finish. What makes it so amazing?"

I rubbed my temples. "I'm so sorry, Piper, but I have a headache. I think I'm going to shut the shop a little early. You can go on home."

Hurt and something else flashed in her eyes but she tamped it down. "Of course." She brushed past me and grabbed her purse. "Call me if you need me to come in early tomorrow."

"Of course," I said. "I'll see you around lunch."

She waved and let herself out. As soon as the door shut, my shoulders slumped and a sigh escaped me. It was five minutes until six and there was no one else in the store or coming up the drive. Safe enough to close.

I was just turning the key into the lock when a knock sounded from outside. I peered out only to see Sam there.

"Hey!" I said, surprised to see him. He looked as disheveled as usual, his shaggy hair in complete disarray. He wore a pair of jeans, an old 80s band t-shirt, and a pair of Converse. Perched on his face was a pair of silver wire-rimmed glasses which made him look adorably geeky. My heart tripped on itself as I held the door open. I valued his friendship too much to embarrass myself by flirting with him. For whatever reason, Sam was staunchly single and wanted to stay that way.

He pushed his glasses up with a finger. "I think I found something." Sam walked in as I held the door open and brushed past, leaving behind the scent of books and coffee.

"I'm just shutting everything down so can you give me a couple more minutes?" I asked as I shut the door. "There's a coffee pot in the kitchen if you want to make some or bottled water in the fridge. Just make yourself at home."

"Okay," he said and wandered off. An amused smile lit my lips as he disappeared from view. I guess he was the kind of person to take a statement like that literally, but I wasn't worried. I grabbed the broom and did a quick sweep of the front area, adjusting the soaps back to their original spot as I passed by them. It took less than ten minutes before everything was tidy, and I was just putting the broom away when there was another knock on the door.

I stilled, wondering who it could be. Peeking out the window, I saw Sloane standing there, his arms full of bags. He was thirty minutes early.

I opened the door and reached out to take one of his bags. "You're early," I accused, but I wasn't mad.

"Sorry," he said sheepishly. "I thought this was too important to wait and I knew you closed at six."

"Come on in. You can set everything down on the counter." I followed behind him, staring at the load in his arms dubiously. It seemed like a lot just for a few cameras. When he finished setting everything down, Sam came out of the kitchen holding two steaming mugs of coffee. He stopped upon seeing Sloane.

"Oh! Would you like a cup of coffee? I only have

two hands, but I can bring one more." Sam's expression was curious, but he didn't ask why Sloane was here.

The officer stilled, his gaze taking in the cozy scene. I chewed my lip and wondered if I should break the silence. Nothing had happened here, nor would it, but there was something awkward here.

"Have you met Sam?" I asked. "He's the Moonmist librarian and a friend of mine." I smiled encouragingly at Sam as I took the mug from him.

"I haven't," Sloane said. He made sure nothing was going to fall off the counter before he stuck his hand out. "I'm Sloane Kramer." It was obvious what he did because he was still in his uniform. "I'm brand new to the police department."

A friendly smile lit Sam's face up. "Nice to meet you then! Welcome to Moonmist." He eyed Sloane's uniform. "I'm glad they're beefing up the police force. It's better to do that too soon than too late!" They shook hands and Sam started to eye the bags. "What's all this?" He peeked in and when he saw what it was, one of his eyebrows rose. "Everything okay, Ivy?"

I opened my mouth to tell him everything was fine, but Sloane jumped in, to my surprise.

"Ivy thinks something might be going on around

here. She had some things stolen from her shop, so I suggested installing the camera at least for a little while."

An adorable crinkle in Sam's brow formed before he nodded. "Good idea. You need help installing these?"

And that's how two strangers instantly bonded. Over my stress. I shook my head and let them bond over manly installation techniques while I wandered into the kitchen and rummaged through the fridge for something to cook for dinner.

Harry wandered out while I was cooking the ground beef. "Oh, if I only had taste buds!" he lamented. "What are you making?" He leaned over the pot and examined it.

"Beef stroganoff."

"Realllllyyy?" he drawled. "It doesn't look traditional," he said in an imperious tone.

"It's not," I said and slapped his bony fingers with the wooden spoon when he was about to stick them inside of the pan. "It's an American and Russian mashup. No red wine or beef fillet. It has white wine and ground beef. Plus Worcestershire and mustard." I added a little flour to the pan and stirred it into the beef, mushroom, and onion mixture. "It's delicious." I hadn't made it in a long time, but I was feeling the need for comfort food.

It wasn't a dish I made often anymore because it was way more than I could eat at one time. Since I had two guests here this evening, they could take some of it home or eat it here after they were finished setting everything up. Both of them had disappeared deeper into the house. Sloane told me they planned to put cameras in my workshop and in the store portion of the house - both places where Piper would have a reason to be.

I added the egg noodles and the rest of the seasonings to the stroganoff and put a lid over the pot so it could finish cooking. I grabbed a towel to wipe my hands and headed to the workshop to see the progress.

Sloane and Sam stood with their backs to me, staring up at the corner of the wall.

"I dunno," Sam said. "I can see it."

"But if you didn't know it was there could you see it?" Sloane asked.

I leaned against the door and crossed my arms over my chest. "I can't see it." I peered up at the corner where they were staring. I saw a small black dot but that was it. It almost looked like a spider or something.

"Well," I clarified, "I can see something, but I

wouldn't think it was a camera if I happened to glance up."

"That's what I said!" Sloane turned to look at me. "Something smells delicious."

"Stroganoff," I said as I pushed off the wall and came to stand beside them. "There will be extra if you both want some."

"I'd love some," Sloane and Sam said at the same time.

"How many cameras did you have to put in here?" I asked as I looked around. I could only see one, but I probably wouldn't have noticed it if I hadn't seen them looking at it.

"Just two," Sam said. "The one you just saw takes care of most of the room, but there was an angle we couldn't get in the shot, so we added one more just to make sure we got the entire room."

"And in the store?" I said, still trying to find the other camera.

"Three," Sloane said. "Two in the store and one outside pointing toward the parking lot. We've tested everything and it looks like it's all working." Sloane scratched his chin. "Of course, if you want to keep it up and running once this is all over, I'd probably suggest a different system. I'm not an expert by any means, and I'm sure there are a lot more systems out there better than what we just rigged up."

I shrugged. "Considering I didn't have anything before this, I'm sure it's fine." I tilted my head toward the kitchen and the timer went off as soon as I did. "Come get a bowl of stroganoff while it's hot. Then you can teach me how to operate everything."

The men followed me back and I thought about how weird it was to have both of them in my house at the same time. Of course, I felt safe for the first time since this had all happened, but a pang of loneliness hit me, too. Maybe I should try getting out there more. I pulled the sour cream from the fridge and plopped about half a cup into the pot. I turned off the heat and stirred it in. Once I adjusted the salt and pepper, I grabbed two large bowls and scooped a bunch in for Sam and Sloane. Once I had mine, I snagged one of the stools and plopped down. Sam and Sloane sat at the kitchen table.

Harry came in and dramatically dropped down on the couch, leading to an amused glance from Sam. I rolled my eyes and was about to say something when the doorbell rang. As soon as I opened the door, Lacey ran into the house. Charlie laughed. "She must smell something really good in there."

I heard the pup yipping with delight. "She's never met a man she didn't like," I said dryly.

"She is super friendly," he said. "That's a good thing. I'll pick her up in three days?"

I nodded. "I have the list, so I'll make sure I keep up with her training."

"Good," Charlie said, "because I just told her to sit when you opened the door."

We both laughed and I waved goodbye. When I walked back into the kitchen, both Sam and Sloane were on the floor showering Lacey with attention.

Be still my beating heart. There were fewer things cuter than a man with a puppy. Harry stared at the three of them, his head propped up on his hand. I knew he was waiting to see what Sam had found out, but I thought he might be disappointed because Harry wouldn't tell Sam anything about what he remembered.

I picked my stroganoff back up and polished it off while the men played with Lacey.

SLOANE AND SAM both washed their dishes before they beckoned me over to my laptop. "If you want to turn the cameras on," Sloane said, "you just press this button." He hovered the mouse over it and clicked. "To turn it off, you click it again." He then showed me how to access past footage and told me to call him if I had any problems. "I set it up for only you to be able to access it, but if there's an emergency, you can press a button in the app to call the police." He asked for my cell phone and downloaded something to it while I watched. Sloane opened the app and showed me how to report an emergency.

Technology was something.

I thanked both men profusely, even though Sam wasn't supposed to be involved in it. Sloane headed out and promised to check in tomorrow. Sam lingered on the porch and when Sloane was gone asked to see Harry.

I called for the spirit and he clomped outside with us. Sam greeted him.

"I did some more digging and thought I had something for you, but now that I talked to Sloane, I'm almost positive I'm correct."

Harry almost vibrated with excitement.

"Mind you," Sam continued, "it would be helpful if you gave us any information you can, but in the absence of it, I have to say I think you are either a trapped spirit just like Ivy thought, or you're a trapped soul. I could tell you for sure if you'd divulge the information you're hanging on to. I can't help you if you don't because the magic to release a spirit versus a soul is very different from each other."

Harry stood stock still, but his eyes flared purple. I took a step back and stared at the animated skeleton. Just because he'd always been harmless didn't mean he was always harmless.

"I see," Harry said. "You've given me a lot to think about. Thank you for investigating." Without waiting for Sam to respond, Harry turned and went back inside.

When he was sure Harry was out of hearing range, Sam spoke again. "Ivy, I think he's a spirit and not a soul. They're two different things. If it's a spirit, he could be extremely dangerous if released."

"What do you mean? Spirits can't form bodies can they?"

Sam's hair glinted with gold underneath the dim porch lights. "No, but they can possess people. That makes it infinitely worse." He sighed. "And I'm afraid I might have given him the information he needs."

"You didn't tell him anything," I argued.

"I narrowed it down to two things. There's a 50/50 chance he'll get it right." He stared back into the house. "You don't have any other books in there that could help him figure this out, do you?"

I thought about it. "Just the ones from the library.

But Harry has access to the internet. You don't think that's an issue, do you?"

Sam chuckled. "I can't get over the image of a skeleton using the internet. I'm not sure. I don't think the internet will have the spell he needs to be able to undo what's been done to him, but you never know when he might connect with someone who does. I'd be careful to continue to monitor this. It's not something I'd ignore."

I sighed. "I don't feel comfortable with all this spying."

"It isn't spying," Sam argued. "Not really."

I crossed my arms over my chest and looked at him.

"Fine," he admitted. "Probably. But if you don't, you might be in a world of trouble if he figures out how to get out from his prison." Worry wafted from him, strong and rich.

I looked back toward the house, my mouth turned down in a frown. "Harry has never given me any trouble."

"Because he's limited to what he can do," Sam said, his voice getting frustrated. "You said he can't go past the perimeters of the land right now. I think it's because there's some sort of lock on his powers. If he's an actual spirit, he has powers. And a lot of them, potentially." He touched my arm. "Please. Just think about it."

After a moment, I nodded. "Thank you for your help." I didn't have the time or mental capacity to think about Harry right now. I had a potential murderer working for me. One thing at a time.

"My pleasure," Sam said. "Thanks for feeding me dinner. It's been a long time since I've had a home-cooked meal."

"I enjoy cooking. I was glad to do it." I watched as Sam headed down the steps and waved at him when he got into his car. I didn't go back inside right away. Instead, I took a seat in the rocking chair on the porch and breathed in the fresh air. I had a feeling things around here were about to be solved whether I wanted them to or not.

I was afraid things might never be the same when they were.

14

—————

Things were uneventful for the majority of the day, though I walked around the store nervous as a cat trying to avoid a room full of rocking chairs. I felt fidgety and nervous, and I thought even Piper noticed it because I caught her looking at me with a strange expression a few times. I excused myself a couple of hours after she got there. First, I needed a break and second, I wanted to see if my neurotic suspicions were correct. Not that she would do anything today, but I knew for sure she wouldn't do anything while I was there.

I grabbed my purse. "I have to run out for a few hours," I said. "Are you okay with holding down the ship while I'm gone?"

"Of course," Piper said, her cheery smile a touch too bright. "Everything okay with you?"

"I'm fine. I've just had a couple of nights of poor sleep." I smiled at her. "I'll have my cell on so call me if you need anything. I'll try to be back before closing, but I can't guarantee it."

"No problem," Piper assured me. "I'll take care of it."

"Thanks." I snagged my keys and headed out the door, doing my best to pretend to be carefree. The last thing I needed was her being suspicious of me. I made sure I had my phone with me because I could monitor the cameras remotely if I needed to.

As soon as I was in the car and driving toward downtown, I let out a slow breath. I wasn't good at subterfuge. I never had been. There were no errands I needed to run. I just needed to get out of the store. I drove aimlessly for a while before I turned down my sister Rose's street. I noticed her car wasn't in the drive, so I continued driving and eventually found myself at her office. Rose had odd work hours. I guess predicting and controlling the weather didn't come with banker's hours.

I found her with several other people drinking coffee and looking at maps spread out all over the table. Her twins were at a separate table close to

Rose and finger painting on a large sheet of rolled out paper. That seemed dangerous indeed considering Rose didn't have her eyes on them every second the paint was out, but it wasn't my office to watch.

Her face lit with surprised delight when she saw me. "Ivy!" she exclaimed. "What are you doing here?"

"Just thought I'd pop by for a little bit. I had some free time from the store." I peered down at the maps. "What are you doing? Planning summer?"

Rose laughed and pulled me forward. "Hey everyone! Most of you know Ivy, but if you don't, this is my sister."

I waved at them all. I knew most of them, but there were a couple of people I'd never seen before. I wasn't surprised. This job didn't have longevity for a lot of people because it could be stressful. You were fighting against natural weather patterns and it required a lot of patience, a lot of magic, and the ability to analyze weather. I once heard meteorology was one of the most difficult careers to get into and looking at all the maps and paperwork scattered around their table, I could see how it was probably true.

"Hey Ivy!" a few called back. Rose took me by the

elbow and called back, "Can you keep an eye on them for me for a minute?"

"Sure thing!" a woman said.

She pulled me out of the room and down the hall. When she was satisfied we were alone, she peered at me, concern in her gray eyes. "What's wrong?"

I sighed. "Why do you automatically think something is wrong?"

"Because you never come visit me at work and your eyes look haunted. Like you haven't slept in a week. What's going on?"

I looked around before I spoke. "I think Piper might have had something to do with Michael Harper's murder." Last night I didn't want to think about it, but the pieces of it all had arranged themselves in my head and all clues were pointing back to her.

Rose gasped in shock. "No. Are you certain?"

I shook my head. "Not certain."

She put her index finger over her lips and gestured for me to follow her. A few moments later, she shut her office door. "Sit down and tell me everything."

. . .

AN HOUR HAD PASSED before I'd told Rose everything including my suspicions. To her credit, she didn't dismiss anything I said. Instead, she shook her head and pursed her lips. "I can't believe it. I never would have expected Piper to be involved in any of this."

My phone made a noise I'd never heard before. I plucked it out of my purse and stared at it. An alert had popped up from the camera app. I opened it up.

Rose came to stand behind me. "What is it?"

It took a moment to load and when it did, I saw Piper in my workshop, but there was another woman there, too.

Tiffany. The woman who'd ordered lye from Moonmist. Unfortunately, the cameras didn't have sound, but I could see Piper's face.

My assistant looked terrified. "I have to go," I said abruptly. I stood and grabbed my purse.

"I'll come with you!" Rose said. She grabbed her purse and jacket.

"What about the twins?" I said as I held the door open for her.

She dialed a number on her cell and spoke to whoever was on the other line, ignoring me.

"All taken care of," she said a moment later. "Let me take my car. That way Piper won't know you're back."

We climbed in and headed back to the store.

I REACHED up and grabbed the bell over the door before it could alert Piper to our presence. It hadn't taken long to get back - a matter of minutes, but a lot could happen in that short a time. Rose had gone around to the back of the house and waited out there just in case things went wrong. I told her if I wasn't out in five minutes or less to contact the police. I didn't know what was going on, but Piper knew she wasn't allowed to let anyone in my work-shop. Ever.

There were no signs of Harry anywhere in the house which was also concerning. I tiptoed through the house and stopped outside of the workshop. They were still in there and their voices were raised.

"I can't give you anything else," Piper said, a pleading note in her voice. "I think she's on to me."

"I don't care if she is. I need those recipes, Piper," the other woman said. "She's making a lot of money here and I want in on it. If I can get her recipes, I can edge her out of business."

I almost snorted at the words. "A lot of money" and "soap maker" were rarely used in the same sentence. I was doing okay, but my business was still brand new and people were still discovering me. I had a while before I could afford to pay myself a real salary. I was fortunate that I'd been left one of the family homes because trying to pay rent on a shop would have bankrupted me.

"Look at this place," the woman sneered. "There must be a lot of money wrapped up in all these supplies and her recipes."

I heard papers rustling around and anger filled me. They were going through my recipes.

"Please," Piper said, "you don't have to do this."

"You were so eager at first," the woman said. "All I had to do was offer you a little money and you were game to give your boss' secret away."

"That was before," Piper whimpered.

"Before I hurt that man?" the woman said. She scoffed. "I had no choice."

I stood up straight at that one. Carefully, I pulled my phone out and opened up the camera app. I couldn't wait on Rose to call the police. They needed to be here as soon as possible. I pressed the button for emergency services and the app made a dinging noise.

I froze, horrified I'd just given myself away.

The two women fell silent.

"What was that?" Tiffany asked.

"This is an old house," Piper said. "Probably just the wind."

Piper was lying. I could smell it in the air. Her worry lay over me like a blanket. As much as I hated what she did, I knew Piper wouldn't hurt anyone intentionally.

"I'm going to check," Tiffany said.

I looked around frantically, but I was in the hallway. There was nowhere to run without her seeing me, so I straightened up and walked right into the shop. Foolhardy? More than likely. But it was the only way I could salvage this.

I pasted on a bright smile and let it fall when I saw Tiffany there. "Hi, Piper," I said. I looked at the other woman and frowned. "You remember you aren't supposed to have anyone else in here, right?"

Piper's eyes were wide and frightened. There was a long pause where I thought she wouldn't play along, but finally, she blurted, "Of course. I'm so sorry. She's ah ... um ... a customer who had a problem with her order and she demanded to come back here."

I only had to stall her for a few minutes before the police arrived. "I'm not sure why she needs to be back here, but I can help her." I frowned. "You look familiar. Have we met?"

The woman's eyes narrowed. I looked away and up at the ceiling and quickly looked away but not before Tiffany noticed. She spun and looked up at the corner.

Right where the camera was.

She turned back around, but this time she held a gun in her hand. Piper whimpered in fear. My legs felt like they were jelly. My magic wasn't defensive or offensive. It just was. Being able to discern emotions wouldn't help me now.

"You know," Tiffany accused and took a couple of steps closer to me. I backed away from her and she followed. Out of the corner of my eye, I saw a flash of something but didn't dare to look closer.

"There's no need for violence," I told her calmly. "You're already in enough trouble for Michael Harper. You can walk out of here right now and I'll wait to call the police," I reasoned. "You can leave Moonmist and start somewhere else."

"I'm not going anywhere," she snapped. There was a desperate look to her. "You have something I want."

"My recipes?" I said with a snort. "You're welcome to all of them." It hurt to say that, knowing the time I'd spent in developing everything, but I knew the recipes weren't everything.

My magic was 70% of the value and she had none of it. Never in my life had I been more glad to have kept my magic secret. She would be able to sell the soap she made, but it would never rival mine for effectiveness.

She frowned. "Why are you so eager to get rid of them now?" Tiffany looked over at Piper in suspicion.

"Because they aren't worth our lives." It was the truth. "So take them and leave."

Tiffany laughed. "You sound just like that other guy did. He was so honest and forthright."

My heart hurt that I inadvertently had a hand in his death. I glanced at Piper. Her face was tight and drawn and her eyes were downcast.

"He was," I said quietly, righteous anger filling my veins.

"Yeah well, he picked the wrong time to go to the bathroom," Tiffany said.

"He was here?" I said, my face going pale.

Tiffany smiled, a vicious thing on her face. "He walked in while Piper was going through your recipes and got his nose into our business."

"You killed him," I whispered. "For no reason."

"For every reason!" she shouted. I jerked in response. Her voice sounded like a gunshot.

"It's soap," I pleaded. "I don't understand this. You can figure this out on your own."

She came another step closer, her face scrunched up as she looked at me. "I think I just did," she said.

My heart pounded in my chest as she advanced.

"It's you," she said, her eyes wide. "*You're* the reason for how well your soap sells."

"It's just soap," I said again. "It's a craft. And I'm not doing nearly as well as you think I am."

"Oh yes, you are," she said. She stole a glance at Piper and my blood ran cold.

I looked at my assistance and saw the guilt all over her face. "You -" I swallowed hard. "You've been stealing from me?"

I racked my brain and tried to see where I'd gone wrong. I knew I'd stopped paying attention to a lot of things in my business because I had someone I trusted taking care of the books and coming in to run the shop part-time. Betrayal speared me in the heart as I opened my magic to her. I never allowed my power to be fully open. If it was, I'd be swamped by emotions all the time.

Horror wafted from Piper as well as guilt and fear. How could I have been so wrong about her?

She didn't answer which was answer enough.

Tiffany laughed, a vicious sound in the silence. "Ever since you hired her. I wouldn't let an old man ruin my cash cow, you know?"

Harry stepped into the workshop behind Tiffany and Piper. I kept my face still. I had no idea how he was being so quiet. Normally he sounded like someone crashing around the kitchen when he walked, but now he was quiet, not a creak or rattle to be heard. Unease settled within me and Sam's words came back to me. If he was a spirit, he might be hiding a lot of things from me.

Like magic. Unlike humans, I couldn't usually judge or feel his emotions. But it looked like Harry was here to help and not harm, so I said nothing. I kept Tiffany and Piper talking so he could do whatever he was here to do. I hoped it would be knocking them out or doing something to immobilize them.

"There's no way you can capitalize on my magic," I said. "No one else has it."

Tiffany smiled at me. "You underestimate me." She waved the gun toward the door. "My truck is out front. I want you to walk slow and steady and get into the passenger seat. You understand?"

If I left this house, I'd never get away from her. I nodded, having zero intentions of getting in the van.

"Good," she said. "Now go."

I took a deep breath, squared my shoulders and took a step toward the door. Harry chose that moment to grab one of the massive wooden rowers I used to stir large batches of soap, held it over his head, and brought it crashing down on top of Tiffany's head. Without waiting to see what happened, I threw myself toward Piper.

She screeched and threw her hands up, not even bothering to fight me. I knocked her to the ground and sat on her, unsure of what else to do.

"Make sure you get the gun!" I shouted to Harry.

Moments later, chaos broke out.

The police busted into the shop, Sloane at the front, his gun drawn and his face carefully blank, though his eyes burned with concern. When he rounded the corner and saw us, I almost laughed at how his expression changed into one of incredulity.

He found a skeleton pointing a gun at an unconscious woman and me sitting on top of another who was too scared to move. Sloane shook his head. "Hand me the gun, Harry," Sloane said.

Harry handed it over and clomped over to me, making all the noise in the world now. He crouched down and put a bony hand on my shoulder. "Are you okay?" he asked, his sharp accent warmer than it was.

"I'm okay," I said, though my lower lip wobbled. "Thank you for that. I don't know what would have happened if you hadn't come in."

Sloane and the other officers busied themselves with taking in Tiffany and Piper, though his face darkened noticeably when he saw who I was sitting on.

"I started suspecting Piper weeks ago, but I didn't have any evidence until just recently. The lye thing was really weird, but I remembered a woman coming in who took a large box out with Piper. She said it was a wholesale soap order, so I didn't question it."

"The lye," I said. "They were trying to learn how to make my soaps."

He nodded. "And they would have succeeded if it weren't for us pesky kids."

A laugh bubbled from me at his Scooby-Doo quote. "Anyone ever tell you you watch too much television?"

"You do all the time, Ivy." He watched Sloane examining everything. "He seems nice," he said out of the blue. "I wouldn't object to more male company around here."

A snort escaped me. "I'm still not sure how I feel about him."

He eyed me. "What about Sam? He's a little more refined. Maybe more your taste." He shrugged. "I prefer the big, gruff guy though."

"I'm not dating anyone right now," I said with a sigh. "They're both nice, but I have too much going on." A dark frown crossed my face. "I have to figure out how much money I've been bleeding these last few months."

Harry jerked his head in Piper's direction as an officer led her out in handcuffs. "She's wearing five hundred-dollar shoes," he observed.

I shut my eyes. "I wouldn't have known that." I looked down at my beat-up Converse. They had to be at least five years old.

"Too much time on the internet," Harry said. "You wouldn't believe how boring it is to be a skeleton who can't leave the property."

"So ... a lot probably," I said, my shoulders slumped.

"Probably," Harry agreed.

Sloane overheard us and came over. He sat down on the floor. "I'm going to have to get a statement from you." He eyed the door where Piper and Tiffany had disappeared. "If you can figure out how much money was stolen, you can request restitution. You probably won't get all of your money back, but you might get some."

"I'll pull the store transactions." The good thing was I had an electronic system set up to track all the register's sales. I'd never given Piper access to it. A good thing all things considered. "It might take me a while to figure it out."

Sloane grinned. "I'll make sure the wheels of justice run a little slower than normal," he said.

I scrubbed my hands over my face. "It was the cameras," I said. "I got an alert and saw Tiffany in the shop."

"You should have called me first," he said. "I can't express to you how dangerous it was to come back here by yourself. You're lucky Harry was here."

I nodded, feeling miserable. "I know. He was a lifesaver." Harry preened.

Something occurred to me and I sat straight up. "Where's Lacey?"

My sister Rose came back in then, carrying the wriggling pup. An officer stopped her at the door and barred her from entry. Her face was pale until she saw me.

I waved at her and mouthed thank you.

She nodded and gave me a long look before she turned around. "I'll put her outside for a little while," she said. There was no fence, but she'd be okay on a lead for a little while. At least until everyone cleared out. Knowing her, she'd love it, especially with everyone tromping all over the yard right now. Lots of opportunities for belly scratches.

Sloane pulled out his notepad. A sigh escaped me before I could stop it and the ghost of a smile flickered on his mouth before it disappeared. I shifted to get into a more comfortable position.

We were going to be here for a while.

15

———————

I'd never needed a weekend more in my life than I needed it today. I rolled over in bed, blinking at the sunlight streaming in my bedroom window. It was Saturday and I'd closed the store. My workshop was a crime scene right now so I wouldn't be able to use it until they allowed me back in. Thankfully, they'd let me move some of the stock out so I could continue selling.

I'd reopen on Monday morning. This weekend I planned to take it easy, but I also needed to go through my books and figure out what had been taken from me. The events of the last several days flashed through me and I squeezed my eyes shut. Michael Harper had died a senseless death. The entire thing came down to greed and wanting what someone else had without having to work for it. Piper's betrayal stung, but if I thought about it, a lot of it was my fault. Of course, I didn't have any control over whether someone stole from me or hurt someone else, but if I'd paid more attention, I might have stopped this entire thing before it started.

That was what hurt the worst. I rubbed my hands over my face and got out of bed, my steps slow. After I got dressed, I wandered out only to find Harry trying to make coffee. Lacey sat by his feet staring up at him curiously. When she saw me, she padded over and nudged me for a pat. I gave her a good scratch before I asked Harry what he was doing.

He snorted which should have been impossible without a nose. "What does it look like I'm doing, Ivy? I'm making coffee." He stared down at the grounds he was scooping into the filter. "Perhaps badly."

"I can take care of it," I said. "Though I do appreciate your effort."

He sighed and stepped away. "I need to know how to do these things," he grumbled. "Especially since I've been living here rent-free for months now."

"Years," I chided him gently, amused at his apparent crisis of conscience.

"I wasn't awake for most of them," he grumbled.

"I can teach you if you'd like," I offered. "But you don't have any way to support yourself, so I don't expect rent. Plus," I added with a sly smile, "I'm not sure the IRS recognizes a skeleton's right to work."

"Har har," Harry said. "I can do a few things around here, though I draw the line at cleaning up after that thing." He pointed at Lacey who sat on her haunches and whined.

"Oh, don't bother, you little faker," he said to Lacey, though his voice was affectionate.

"How about Monday morning, bright and early, I show you how to make coffee and cook a light breakfast?"

Harry looked at me, his eye sockets flashing purple. "Cooking? As long as you promise to cook most. Since I can't eat it."

"I promise. But I'm definitely showing you how to use the crock-pot. Now that I'm down an assistant, I'll be pulling longer hours in the shop."

Harry's eyes flickered at that and flared orange. "I'm sorry about her, and I'm sorry about Mr. Harper."

My shoulders slumped. "Me too. I just wish I'd paid more attention."

A bony hand landed on my shoulder. "You can't

be responsible for other people's actions. You had nothing to do with what happened to him."

"Didn't I?" I asked, shaking my head as the smell of brewing coffee filled the kitchen. "If I have this power, shouldn't I be using it to prevent things like this?"

Harry shrugged. "Do we have an obligation to anything? How could you have known Piper was planning anything? It isn't your responsibility to monitor someone for subterfuge. If you do, you'll live your life constantly searching for something wrong. I think that would be a stressful way to live."

Harry was right, though it didn't take the sting away from some of the things that had happened lately. I nodded and poured myself a cup of coffee. After I doctored it up, I padded into the living room to drink it in the blissful silence of the morning.

The doorbell rang as soon I'd parked myself on the couch. I groaned and went over to open the door.

Sloane stood there holding a basket.

"Hi," I said, feeling super self-conscious about my pajamas and bed head. I held open the door for him to come in and did my best not to peer into the basket to see what he'd brought.

Sloane set the basket down in the kitchen and pulled off the towel. "I brought these from the bakery downtown. I can't remember the name of it, but she said she knew you and to call her when you got a chance."

"Betty?" I asked. She owned more than the restaurant I'd visited.

"That's it," he said. "I'll trade you a muffin for a cup of coffee."

I peered into the basket to see multiple offerings of muffins - blueberry, cranberry, chocolate chip, and double chocolate. I grabbed a chocolate chip and sank my teeth into it. "Done and done," I said with my mouth full.

Sloane made himself at home and when he had his coffee, he leaned against the counter. "I came over to see how you were doing."

I sipped my coffee and tried to come up with the right words. "Sad. Angry." I sighed. "Michael was a good man and he died because of me."

Sloane shook his head. His eyes glittered. "No. He died because of greed. It's as simple as that. You weren't involved at all."

"But I was," I argued. "He died trying to stop someone from stealing from me."

Sloane put his hand on mine. It was warm and calloused and, most of all, comforting. "And he would have done it for anyone. It's just the kind of person he was, Ivy. You can't blame yourself for this."

I didn't agree and sitting there with him, even in spite of his kind words, I knew it would always be difficult not to think about Michael's death and not find fault within myself over it. But I nodded anyway just to make Sloane feel better. And maybe I felt a little better myself simply sitting there with him, but I knew I had a long way to go.

He left shortly after. I showered, dressed, and packed up a few of those muffins. I bid Harry goodbye and headed over to Michael's home.

His widow answered the door and looked surprised to see me. I handed the muffins over and asked to come in.

"Of course," she said.

She offered me coffee which I accepted and when she brought me a mug, we sat in her living room. On the table rested a picture of her and Michael in better times, his arm slung around her and both of them beaming at the camera.

"I'm assuming the police have already talked to you," I began.

She nodded. "They came by last night. I assume that's why you're here?"

"Yes." I gripped the mug she handed me tightly. "I

just wanted to say how sorry I am. I know I've already said it, but I wanted to come by again and tell you that what happened didn't surprise me in the least. I knew he was a good person. I just wish maybe I'd done something more. Paid more attention."

She reached over and gripped my fingers with her own. "He liked you, Ivy."

"I liked him, too. I can't imagine what you're going through right now, but I want you to know my home is always open to you. My shop as well. If you ever need anything, please come find me."

Surprise flowed from her. "That's quite generous. I appreciate it. And if you need anything, please come see me." She smiled, though it wobbled on her face. "I'm not sure how much longer I'll stay here, but I'll continue to live in Moonmist. I grew up here and I plan to die here."

I didn't want to talk about death for the rest of my life. There had been far too much of that lately. "Which will be a very long time from now." I noticed something sitting by the edge of her fireplace.

A besom. I looked at her with surprise.

"Are you..." my voice trailed off.

She saw where my gaze landed. "A witch?" A smile lit her lips. "I am. Though I don't have anything so fascinating as weather or animal magic. I'm quite good with design."

And as I looked around at her tastefully decorated home, I had to agree with her. I narrowed my eyes and an idea struck me. "With everything that's happened, I thought about redoing the shop. I'm good at soap and bath and body. Not design. I could use someone like you to take a look at the shop and help me rearrange it. And not now, of course. Take all the time you need and when you're ready to do something new, please come see me."

Her face lit up. "Oh wow. That sounds ... amazing. I didn't know what I would do after Michael passed, but that sounds so wonderful. And fun."

"Good." We beamed at each other. I dug in my purse for a business card and set it on the table in front of us. "Call me. Any time."

We said goodbye and as I drove home, happiness filled me. Things would never be the same, but I'd done at least one thing I could to honor Michael's memory. His wife seemed like a wonderful person, and their home was beautiful. Maybe she could help me wipe away Piper's memory so I could make new ones on my own.

I passed by the police station and gave it a little wave just in case Sloane was outside. Just a few blocks down was the library and I swung in to drop off the books I'd borrowed.

Sam stood at the desk talking to no less than three women. His expression seemed slightly frazzled, but he managed to make it look good. I bit back a smile as I approached him, but it broke through when he saw me and his eyes widened with relief.

You could practically hear the women sighing when he walked over to me. I didn't want to touch that with a ten-foot pole. Sam was sweet, but I'd be beating women off of him all the time if he ever asked me out. I laughed when he almost skidded to a stop from rushing over to me. I plopped the books down. "Thanks so much for these. I don't need anything else right now, but I'm sure I'll be back next week."

He began scanning them back in, way more slowly than he should have been. I grinned at him and leaned forward.

"One day, someone is going to catch you and you aren't going to know what to do with yourself."

Sam shook his head. "I think I'm going to hire someone to run the desk. Traffic is up so much I can barely get my research done."

A snicker escaped me. "Have you ever read a rom-com?"

He blinked at me. "What?"

This guy. So clueless. "It's called the fake engagement scenario. Or fake girlfriend," I whispered. "Just pretend you have one. A lot of this will stop."

His brow furrowed, but then his face cleared and a beaming smile appeared. "That's brilliant. I don't know why I didn't think of it."

I shrugged. "Because you're too nice. If this is affecting your work, you need to do something about it. It's harmless. No one has to meet her."

"I could kiss you, Ivy Bradshaw," he murmured under his breath.

I held my index finger up and shook it. "Not me. Some woman on a stock photo site. She won't be demanding and won't mind when you cancel all your dates."

He gave me a devastating grin and my heart flip-flopped. "I'm paying all your late fees for the next six months."

I rolled my eyes and turned to go. "That's an empty offer if I've ever seen one. I never turn books in late."

His chuckle followed me out.

I grinned to myself all the way home and when I got out of the car and saw my little house with the cute little sign outside, tears filled my eyes.

Things might be different for a while and I might have to figure out how to run my business anew, but this was my home.

I belonged here, and I couldn't wait to see what came next.

ABOUT THE AUTHOR

USA Today Bestselling author S.E. Babin is a mom, a wife, and a military veteran. She has a passion for writing books with a paranormal twist filled with heroines you'd like to sit down and drink too much wine with and heroes who love those kind of girls. The recipient of several writing awards, Sheryl is content to keep hammering out fun novels with the shenanigans you've come to know her for. She swears some of those shenanigans have actually happened. Also, she likes writing about herself in third person.

Sheryl's past is pretty simple. She spent way too much time in the library, killing any chance of her becoming a cheerleader or anything even remotely cool. Find her on Facebook at https://www.facebook. com/SEBabin or over on Twitter @hungrybiblio. She loves to hear from readers!

Sign up for the newsletter to hear about her newest releases at sebabin.com.

facebook.com/sebabin

LIAR, LYER PREORDER

Ivy Bradshaw has her hands full. With a bustling soap business, a wise-cracking skeleton with mysterious origins, and a handsome necromancer she can't quite get a bead on, Ivy is desperate for a break.

Perfect time for a murder, wouldn't you say?

But this time, Harry is the prime suspect. When Ivy steps up to defend the animate skeleton and one of her only friends in town, the entire town turns against her. The evidence against him is overwhelming and no one seems to care that Harry is bound to Ivy and can only go where she goes.

Ivy was nowhere near the murder scene, but someone is convinced Harry is guilty and will stop at nothing to bring him down.

With more questions than answers and time

running out, Ivy is forced to dig into Harry's past. And when long-buried answers are finally unveiled, nothing will ever be the same.

There isn't enough soap in the world to scrub Harry's alibi clean enough for him to come out of this unscathed...

www.ingramcontent.com/pod-product-compliance
Lightning Source LLC
Chambersburg PA
CBHW071301190726
48292CB00007B/2640